STONE ARCH BOOKS

a capstone imprint

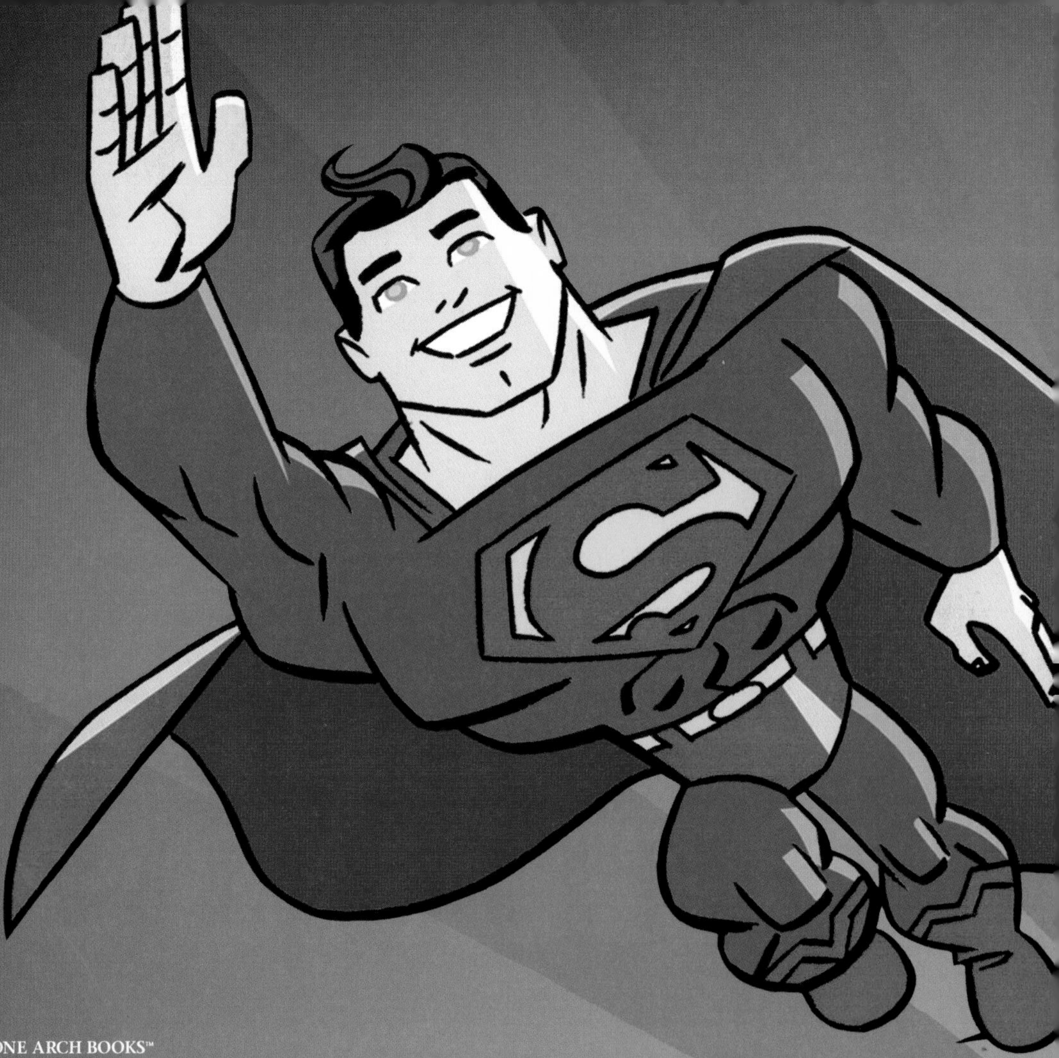

STONE ARCH BOOKS™
Published in 2013
A Capstone Imprint
1710 Roe Crest Drive
North Mankato, MN 56003
www.capstonepub.com

Originally published by DC Comics in
the U.S. in single magazine form as
DC Super Friends #7.

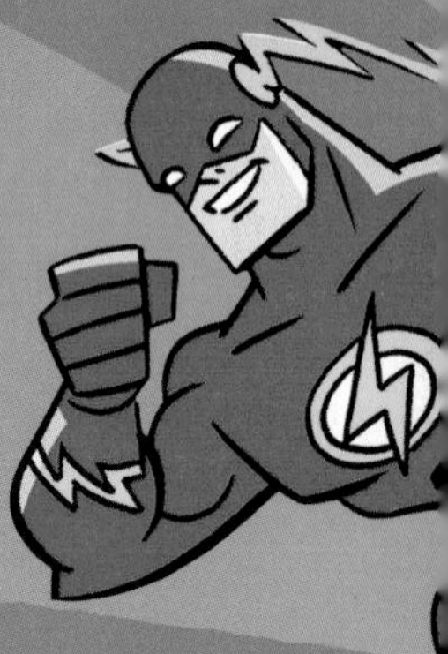

Cataloging-in-Publication Data is available at the
Library of Congress website:
ISBN: 978-1-4342-4702-5 (library binding)

Summary: Amos Fortune believes winning is mostly a
matter of luck - and he's going to make his own from
now on! But the Super Friends bet it takes skill to win.
Who's right?

STONE ARCH BOOKS
Ashley C. Andersen Zantop *Publisher*
Michael Dahl *Editorial Director*
Donald Lemke & Julie Gassman *Editors*
Heather Kindseth *Creative Director*
Brann Garvey *Designer*
Kathy McColley *Production Specialist*

DC COMICS
Rachel Gluckstern *Original U.S. Editor*

Printed in China by Nordica.
1012/CA21201277
092012 006935NORDS13

DC Comics
1700 Broadway, New York, NY 10019
A Warner Bros. Entertainment Company

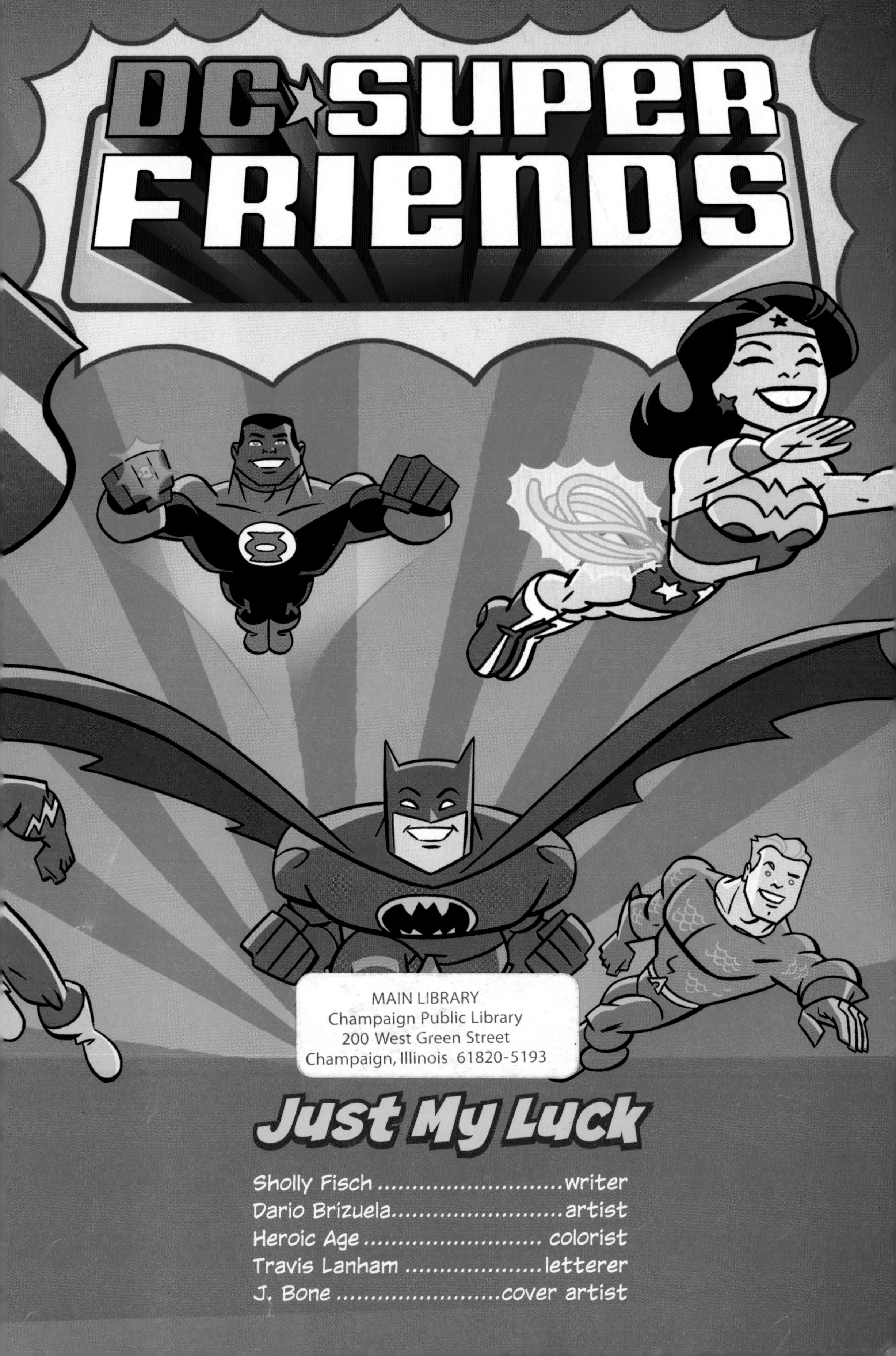
DC SUPER FRIENDS

Just My Luck

Sholly Fisch .... writer
Dario Brizuela .... artist
Heroic Age .... colorist
Travis Lanham .... letterer
J. Bone .... cover artist

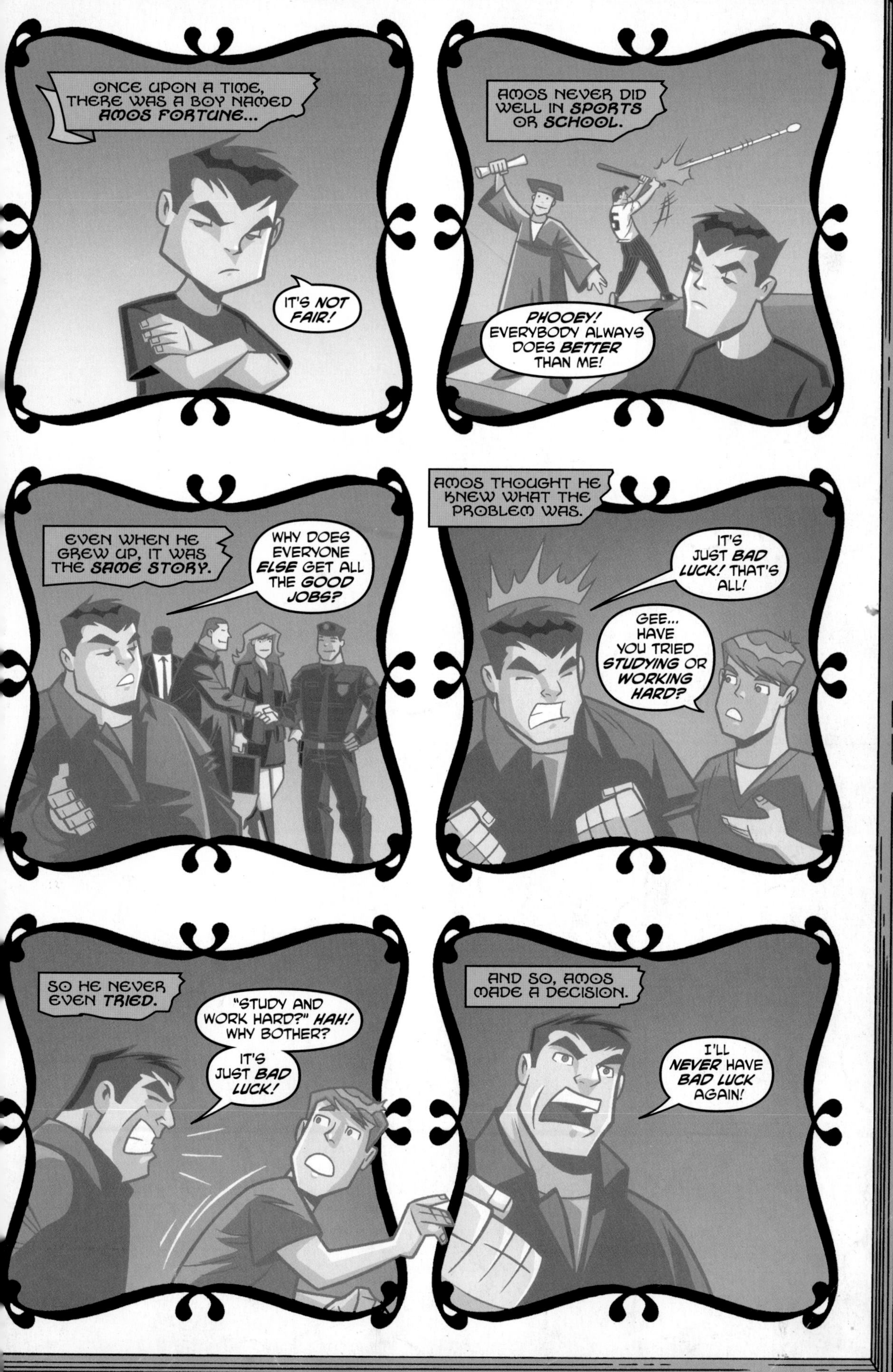
ONCE UPON A TIME, THERE WAS A BOY NAMED AMOS FORTUNE...
IT'S NOT FAIR!
AMOS NEVER DID WELL IN SPORTS OR SCHOOL.
PHOOEY! EVERYBODY ALWAYS DOES BETTER THAN ME!
EVEN WHEN HE GREW UP, IT WAS THE SAME STORY.
WHY DOES EVERYONE ELSE GET ALL THE GOOD JOBS?
AMOS THOUGHT HE KNEW WHAT THE PROBLEM WAS.
IT'S JUST BAD LUCK! THAT'S ALL!
GEE... HAVE YOU TRIED STUDYING OR WORKING HARD?
SO HE NEVER EVEN TRIED.
"STUDY AND WORK HARD?" HAH! WHY BOTHER?
IT'S JUST BAD LUCK!
AND SO, AMOS MADE A DECISION.
I'LL NEVER HAVE BAD LUCK AGAIN!

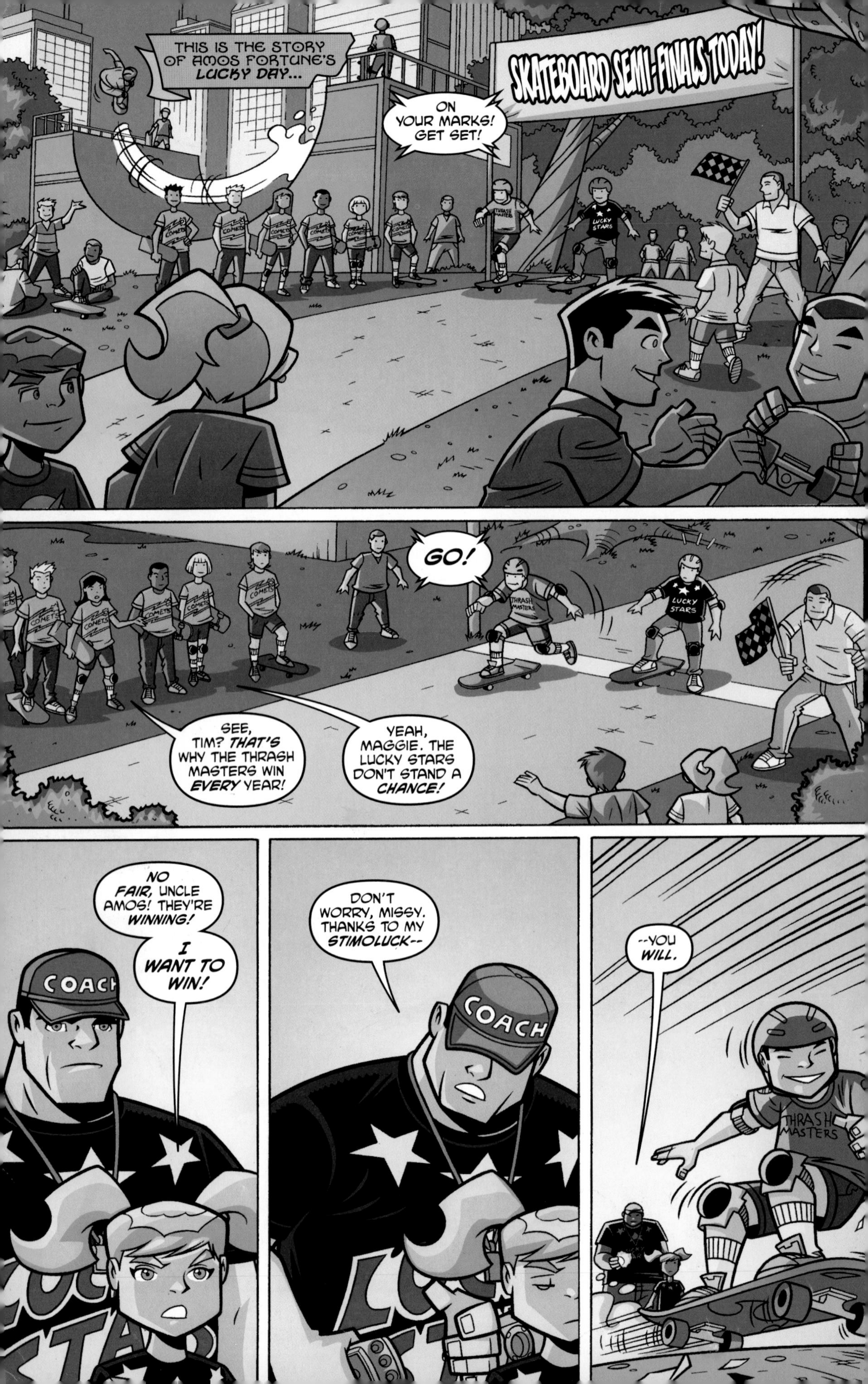
THIS IS THE STORY OF AMOS FORTUNE'S LUCKY DAY...
SKATEBOARD SEMI-FINALS TODAY!
ON YOUR MARKS! GET SET!
COMETS
THRASH MASTERS
LUCKY STARS
GO!
SEE, TIM? THAT'S WHY THE THRASH MASTERS WIN EVERY YEAR!
YEAH, MAGGIE. THE LUCKY STARS DON'T STAND A CHANCE!
NO FAIR, UNCLE AMOS! THEY'RE WINNING!
I WANT TO WIN!
COACH
DON'T WORRY, MISSY. THANKS TO MY STIMOLUCK--
COACH
--YOU WILL.
THRASH MASTERS

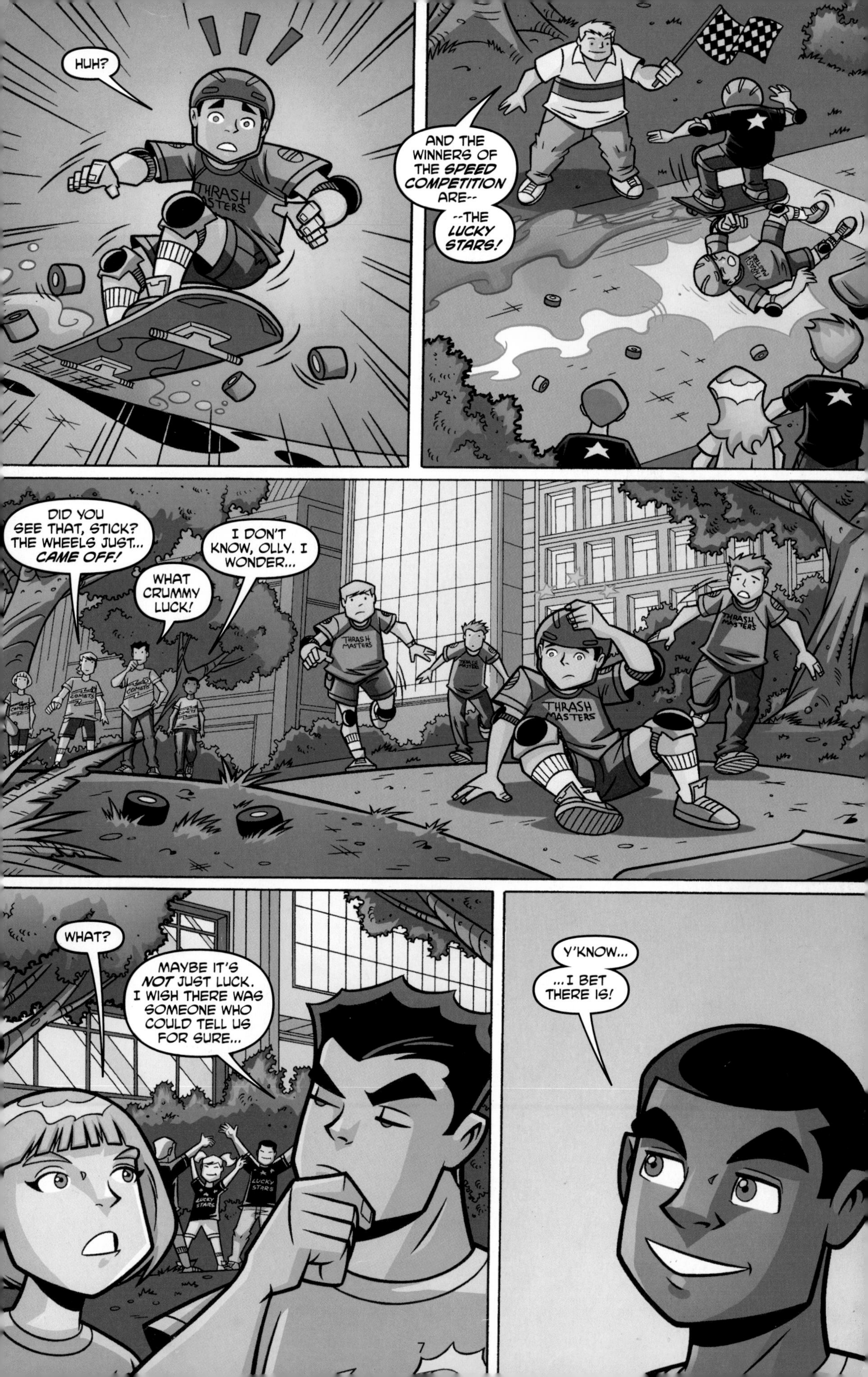
HUH?
AND THE WINNERS OF THE SPEED COMPETITION ARE--
--THE LUCKY STARS!
THRASH MASTERS
DID YOU SEE THAT, STICK? THE WHEELS JUST... CAME OFF!
WHAT CRUMMY LUCK!
I DON'T KNOW, OLLY. I WONDER...
WHAT?
MAYBE IT'S NOT JUST LUCK. I WISH THERE WAS SOMEONE WHO COULD TELL US FOR SURE...
Y'KNOW...
...I BET THERE IS!
LUCKY STARS

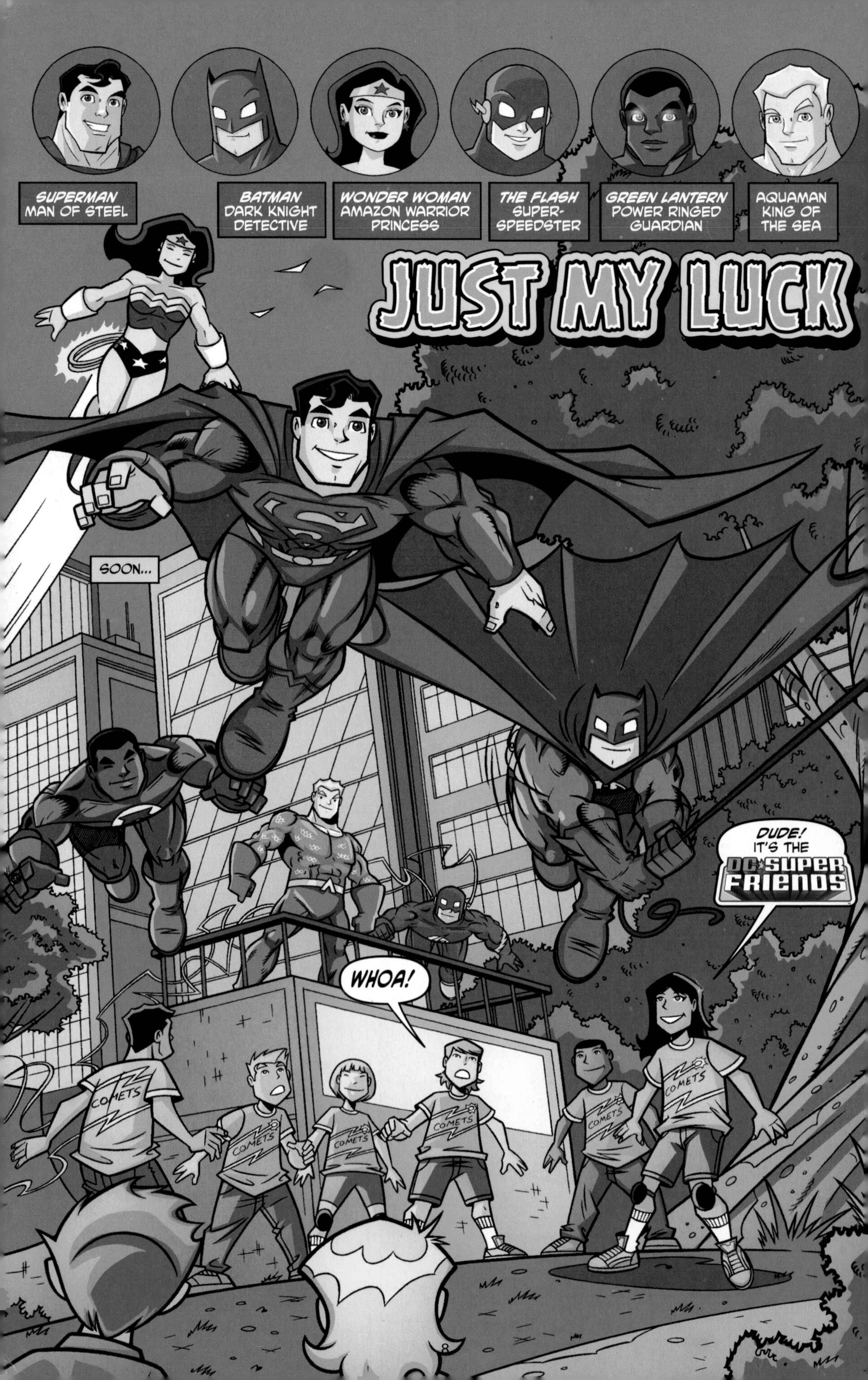
SUPERMAN
MAN OF STEEL
BATMAN
DARK KNIGHT DETECTIVE
WONDER WOMAN
AMAZON WARRIOR PRINCESS
THE FLASH
SUPER-SPEEDSTER
GREEN LANTERN
POWER RINGED GUARDIAN
AQUAMAN
KING OF THE SEA
JUST MY LUCK
SOON...
DUDE! IT'S THE DC SUPER FRIENDS
WHOA!
COMETS

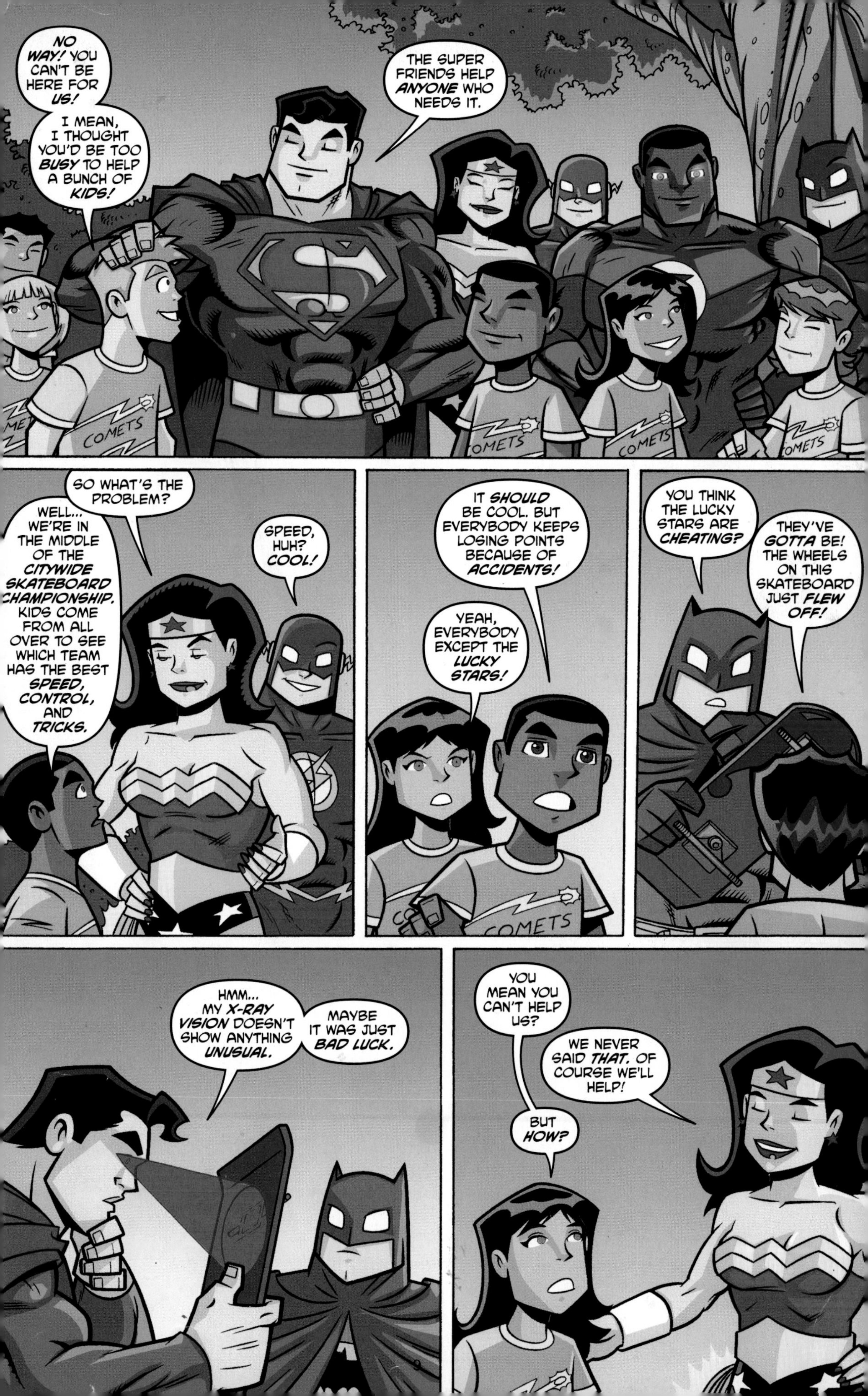
NO WAY! YOU CAN'T BE HERE FOR US!
I MEAN, I THOUGHT YOU'D BE TOO BUSY TO HELP A BUNCH OF KIDS!
THE SUPER FRIENDS HELP ANYONE WHO NEEDS IT.
COMETS
SO WHAT'S THE PROBLEM?
WELL... WE'RE IN THE MIDDLE OF THE CITYWIDE SKATEBOARD CHAMPIONSHIP. KIDS COME FROM ALL OVER TO SEE WHICH TEAM HAS THE BEST SPEED, CONTROL, AND TRICKS.
SPEED, HUH? COOL!
IT SHOULD BE COOL. BUT EVERYBODY KEEPS LOSING POINTS BECAUSE OF ACCIDENTS!
YEAH, EVERYBODY EXCEPT THE LUCKY STARS!
YOU THINK THE LUCKY STARS ARE CHEATING?
THEY'VE GOTTA BE! THE WHEELS ON THIS SKATEBOARD JUST FLEW OFF!
HMM... MY X-RAY VISION DOESN'T SHOW ANYTHING UNUSUAL.
MAYBE IT WAS JUST BAD LUCK.
YOU MEAN YOU CAN'T HELP US?
WE NEVER SAID THAT. OF COURSE WE'LL HELP!
BUT HOW?

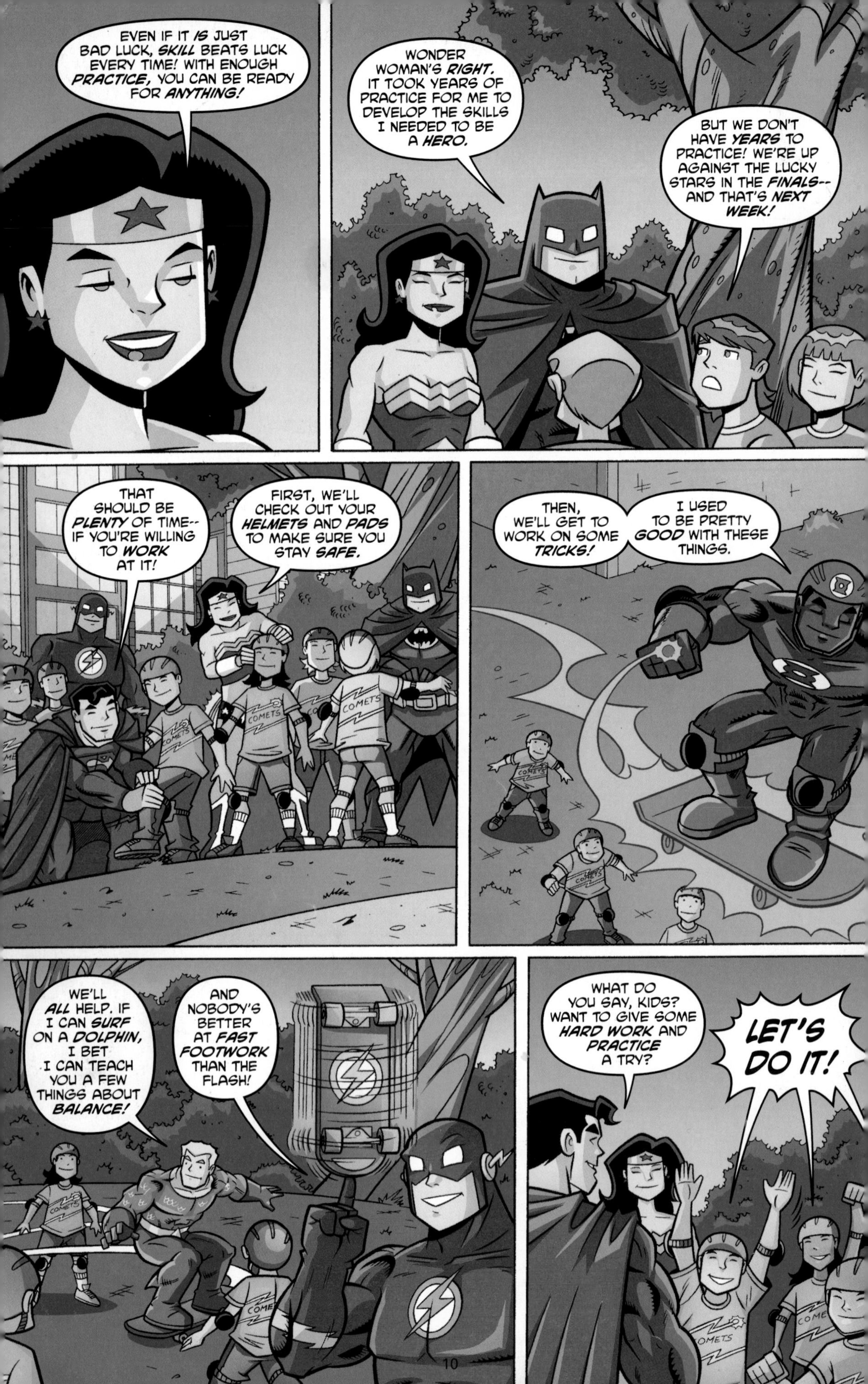
EVEN IF IT IS JUST BAD LUCK, SKILL BEATS LUCK EVERY TIME! WITH ENOUGH PRACTICE, YOU CAN BE READY FOR ANYTHING!
WONDER WOMAN'S RIGHT. IT TOOK YEARS OF PRACTICE FOR ME TO DEVELOP THE SKILLS I NEEDED TO BE A HERO.
BUT WE DON'T HAVE YEARS TO PRACTICE! WE'RE UP AGAINST THE LUCKY STARS IN THE FINALS-- AND THAT'S NEXT WEEK!
THAT SHOULD BE PLENTY OF TIME-- IF YOU'RE WILLING TO WORK AT IT!
FIRST, WE'LL CHECK OUT YOUR HELMETS AND PADS TO MAKE SURE YOU STAY SAFE.
COMETS
THEN, WE'LL GET TO WORK ON SOME TRICKS!
I USED TO BE PRETTY GOOD WITH THESE THINGS.
WE'LL ALL HELP. IF I CAN SURF ON A DOLPHIN, I BET I CAN TEACH YOU A FEW THINGS ABOUT BALANCE!
AND NOBODY'S BETTER AT FAST FOOTWORK THAN THE FLASH!
WHAT DO YOU SAY, KIDS? WANT TO GIVE SOME HARD WORK AND PRACTICE A TRY?
LET'S DO IT!

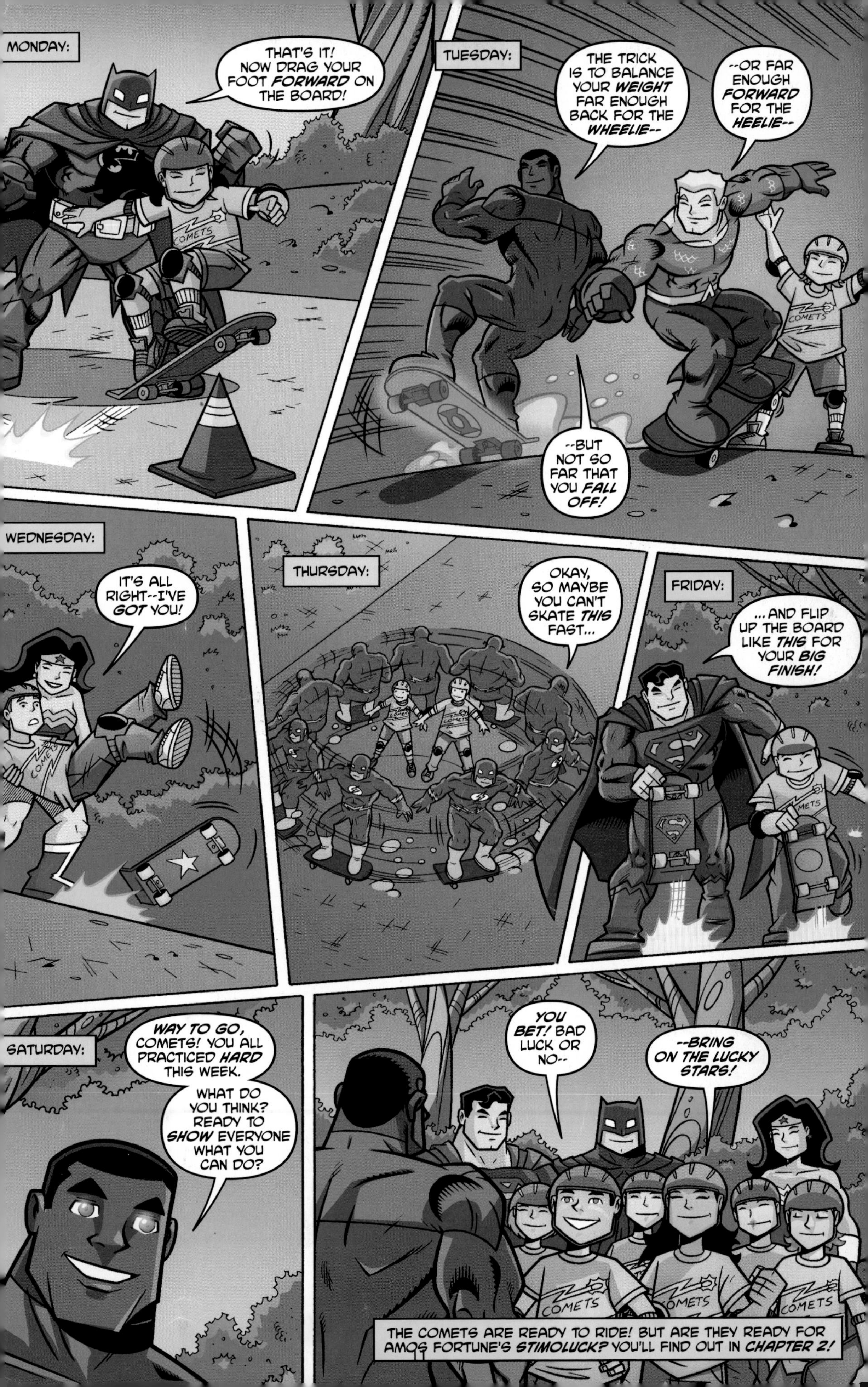
MONDAY:
THAT'S IT! NOW DRAG YOUR FOOT *FORWARD* ON THE BOARD!
TUESDAY:
THE TRICK IS TO BALANCE YOUR *WEIGHT* FAR ENOUGH BACK FOR THE *WHEELIE*--
--OR FAR ENOUGH *FORWARD* FOR THE *HEELIE*--
--BUT NOT SO FAR THAT YOU *FALL OFF!*
COMETS
WEDNESDAY:
IT'S ALL RIGHT--I'VE *GOT* YOU!
THURSDAY:
OKAY, SO MAYBE YOU CAN'T SKATE *THIS* FAST...
FRIDAY:
...AND FLIP UP THE BOARD LIKE *THIS* FOR YOUR *BIG FINISH!*
SATURDAY:
WAY TO GO, COMETS! YOU ALL PRACTICED *HARD* THIS WEEK.
WHAT DO YOU THINK? READY TO *SHOW* EVERYONE WHAT YOU CAN DO?
YOU BET! BAD LUCK OR NO--
--BRING ON THE LUCKY STARS!
THE COMETS ARE READY TO RIDE! BUT ARE THEY READY FOR AMOS FORTUNE'S *STIMOLUCK?* YOU'LL FIND OUT IN *CHAPTER 2!*

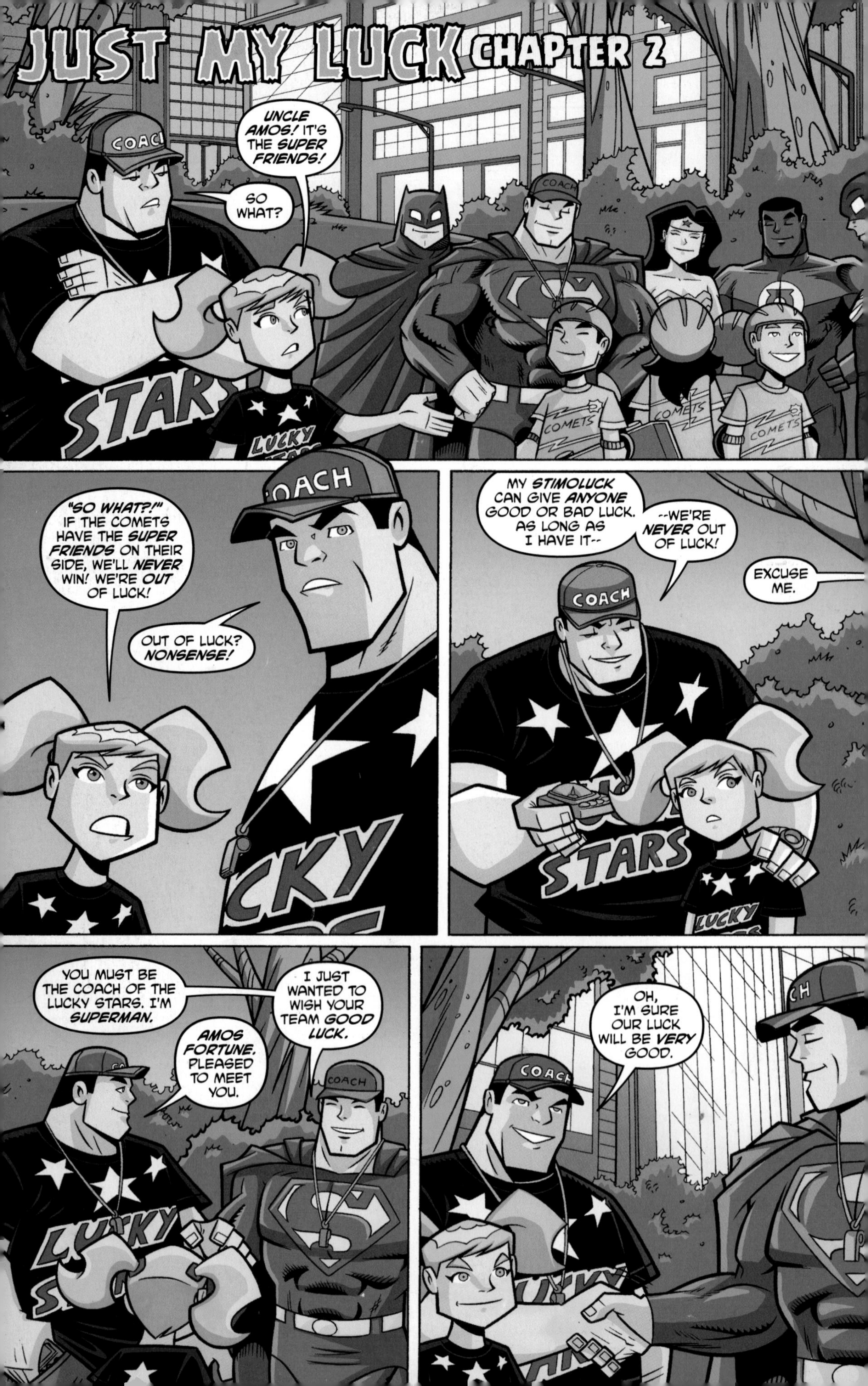
JUST MY LUCK CHAPTER 2
UNCLE AMOS! IT'S THE SUPER FRIENDS!
SO WHAT?
"SO WHAT?!" IF THE COMETS HAVE THE SUPER FRIENDS ON THEIR SIDE, WE'LL NEVER WIN! WE'RE OUT OF LUCK!
OUT OF LUCK? NONSENSE!
MY STIMOLUCK CAN GIVE ANYONE GOOD OR BAD LUCK. AS LONG AS I HAVE IT--
--WE'RE NEVER OUT OF LUCK!
EXCUSE ME.
YOU MUST BE THE COACH OF THE LUCKY STARS. I'M SUPERMAN.
I JUST WANTED TO WISH YOUR TEAM GOOD LUCK.
AMOS FORTUNE. PLEASED TO MEET YOU.
OH, I'M SURE OUR LUCK WILL BE VERY GOOD.

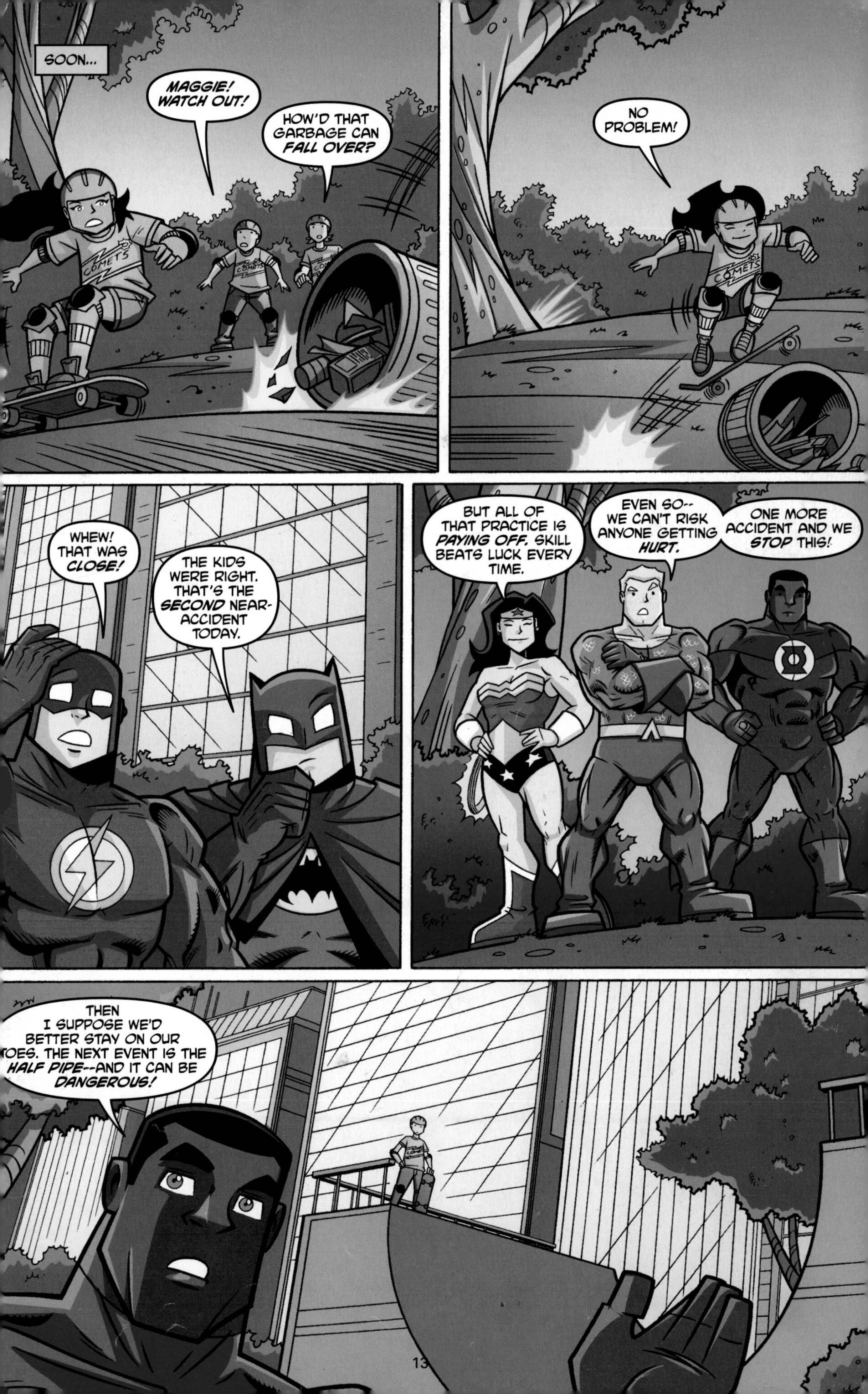
SOON...
MAGGIE! WATCH OUT!
HOW'D THAT GARBAGE CAN FALL OVER?
NO PROBLEM!
WHEW! THAT WAS CLOSE!
THE KIDS WERE RIGHT. THAT'S THE SECOND NEAR-ACCIDENT TODAY.
BUT ALL OF THAT PRACTICE IS PAYING OFF. SKILL BEATS LUCK EVERY TIME.
EVEN SO-- WE CAN'T RISK ANYONE GETTING HURT.
ONE MORE ACCIDENT AND WE STOP THIS!
THEN I SUPPOSE WE'D BETTER STAY ON OUR TOES. THE NEXT EVENT IS THE HALF PIPE--AND IT CAN BE DANGEROUS!
COMETS

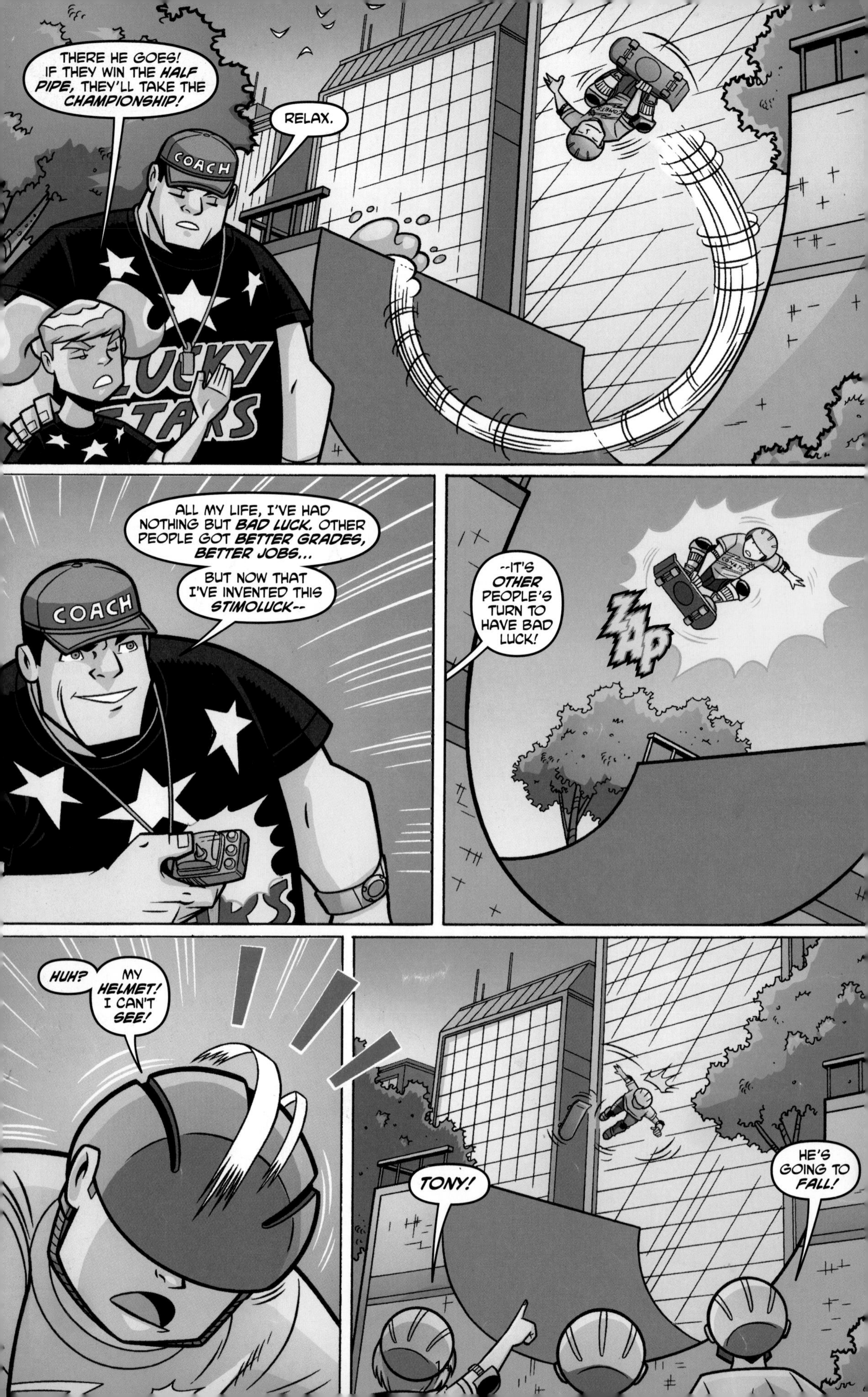
THERE HE GOES! IF THEY WIN THE *HALF PIPE*, THEY'LL TAKE THE *CHAMPIONSHIP!*
RELAX.
COACH
LUCKY STARS
ALL MY LIFE, I'VE HAD NOTHING BUT *BAD LUCK.* OTHER PEOPLE GOT *BETTER GRADES, BETTER JOBS...*
BUT NOW THAT I'VE INVENTED THIS *STIMOLUCK--*
COACH
--IT'S *OTHER* PEOPLE'S TURN TO HAVE BAD LUCK!
ZAP
HUH?
MY *HELMET!* I CAN'T *SEE!*
TONY!
HE'S GOING TO *FALL!*

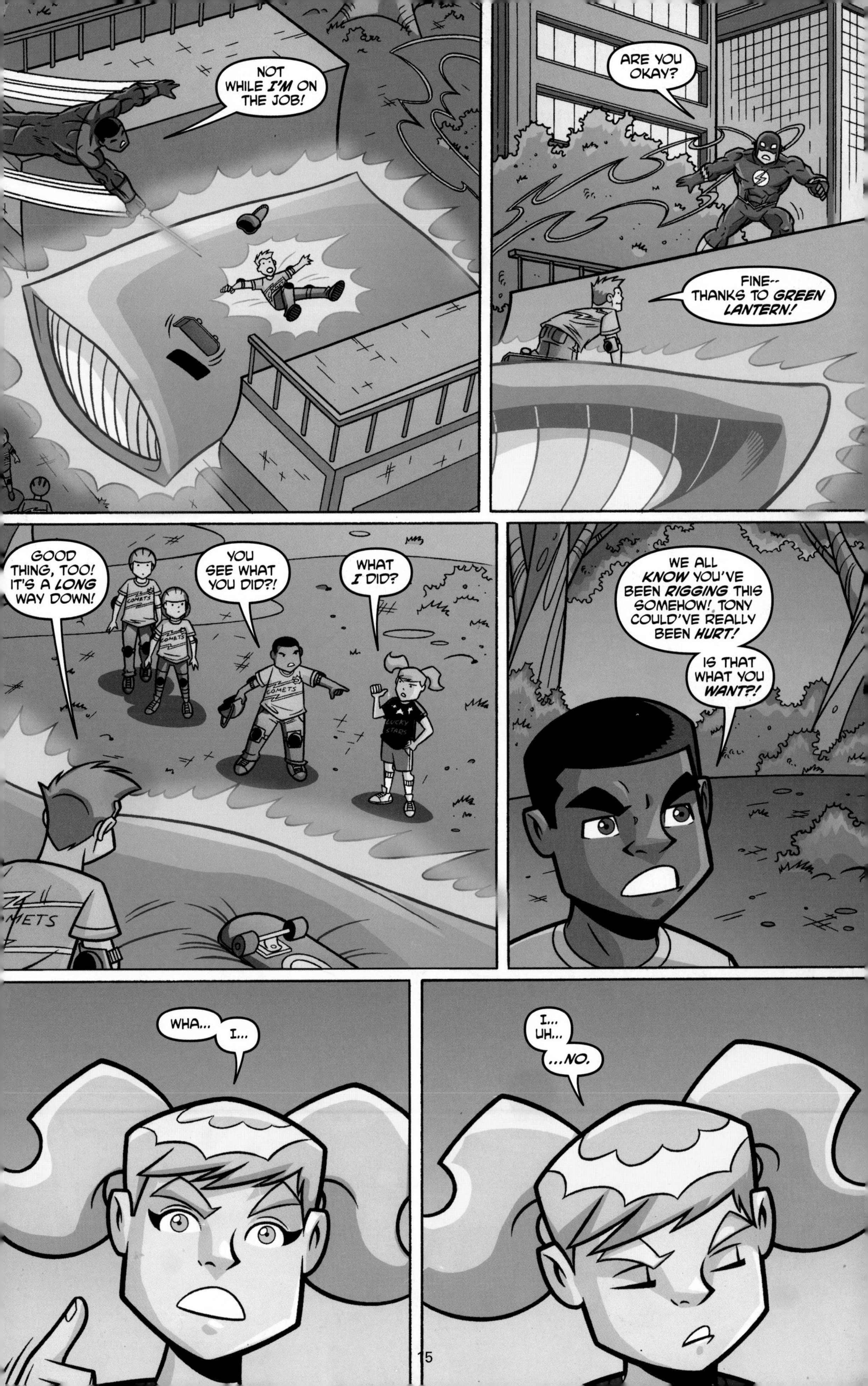
NOT WHILE I'M ON THE JOB!
ARE YOU OKAY?
FINE-- THANKS TO GREEN LANTERN!
GOOD THING, TOO! IT'S A LONG WAY DOWN!
YOU SEE WHAT YOU DID?!
WHAT I DID?
WE ALL KNOW YOU'VE BEEN RIGGING THIS SOMEHOW! TONY COULD'VE REALLY BEEN HURT!
IS THAT WHAT YOU WANT?!
WHA...
I...
I... UH...
...NO.

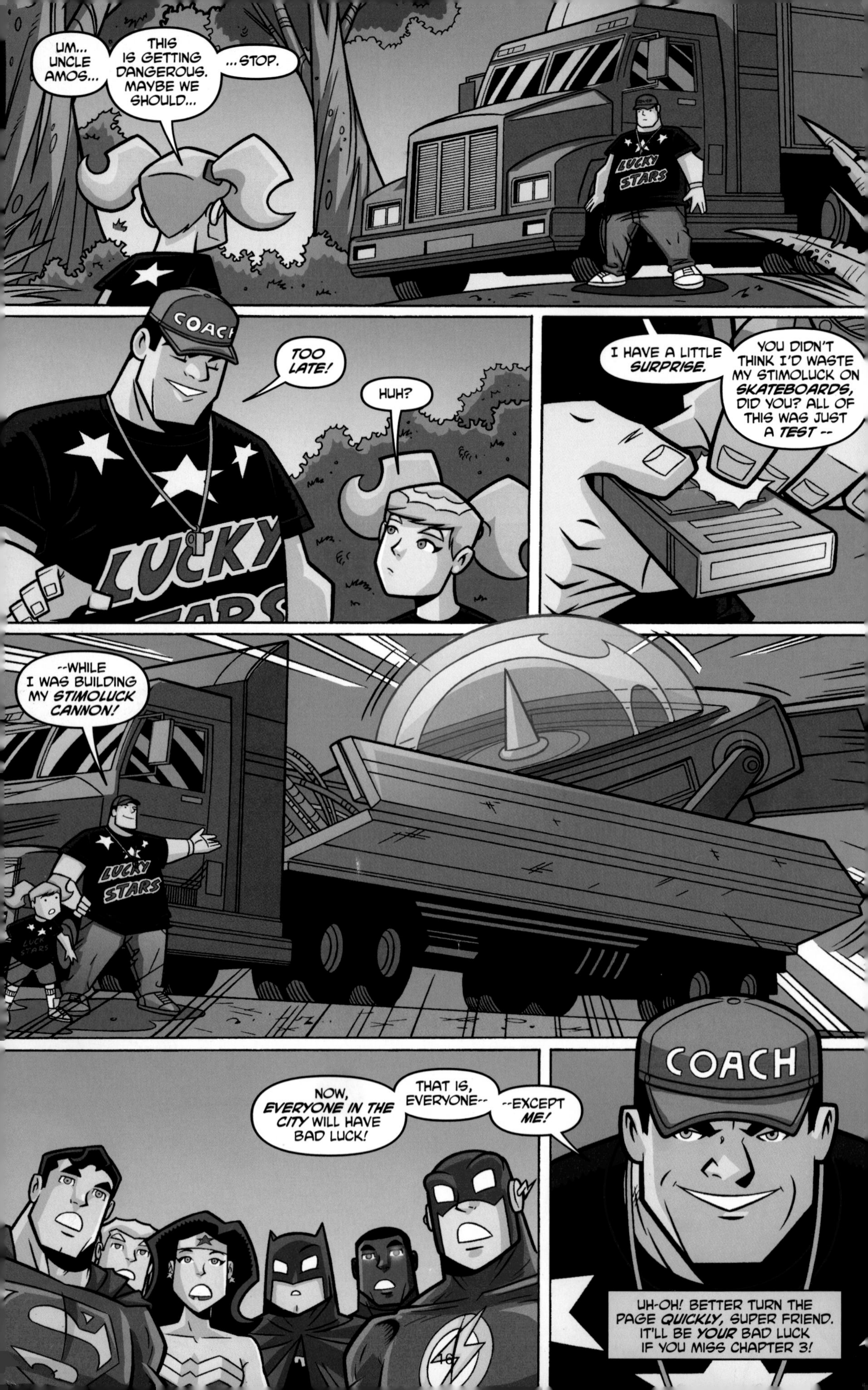
UM... UNCLE AMOS...
THIS IS GETTING DANGEROUS. MAYBE WE SHOULD...
...STOP.
LUCKY STARS
COACH
TOO LATE!
HUH?
LUCKY STARS
I HAVE A LITTLE SURPRISE.
YOU DIDN'T THINK I'D WASTE MY STIMOLUCK ON SKATEBOARDS, DID YOU? ALL OF THIS WAS JUST A TEST --
--WHILE I WAS BUILDING MY STIMOLUCK CANNON!
LUCKY STARS
NOW, EVERYONE IN THE CITY WILL HAVE BAD LUCK!
THAT IS, EVERYONE--
--EXCEPT ME!
COACH
UH-OH! BETTER TURN THE PAGE QUICKLY, SUPER FRIEND. IT'LL BE YOUR BAD LUCK IF YOU MISS CHAPTER 3!

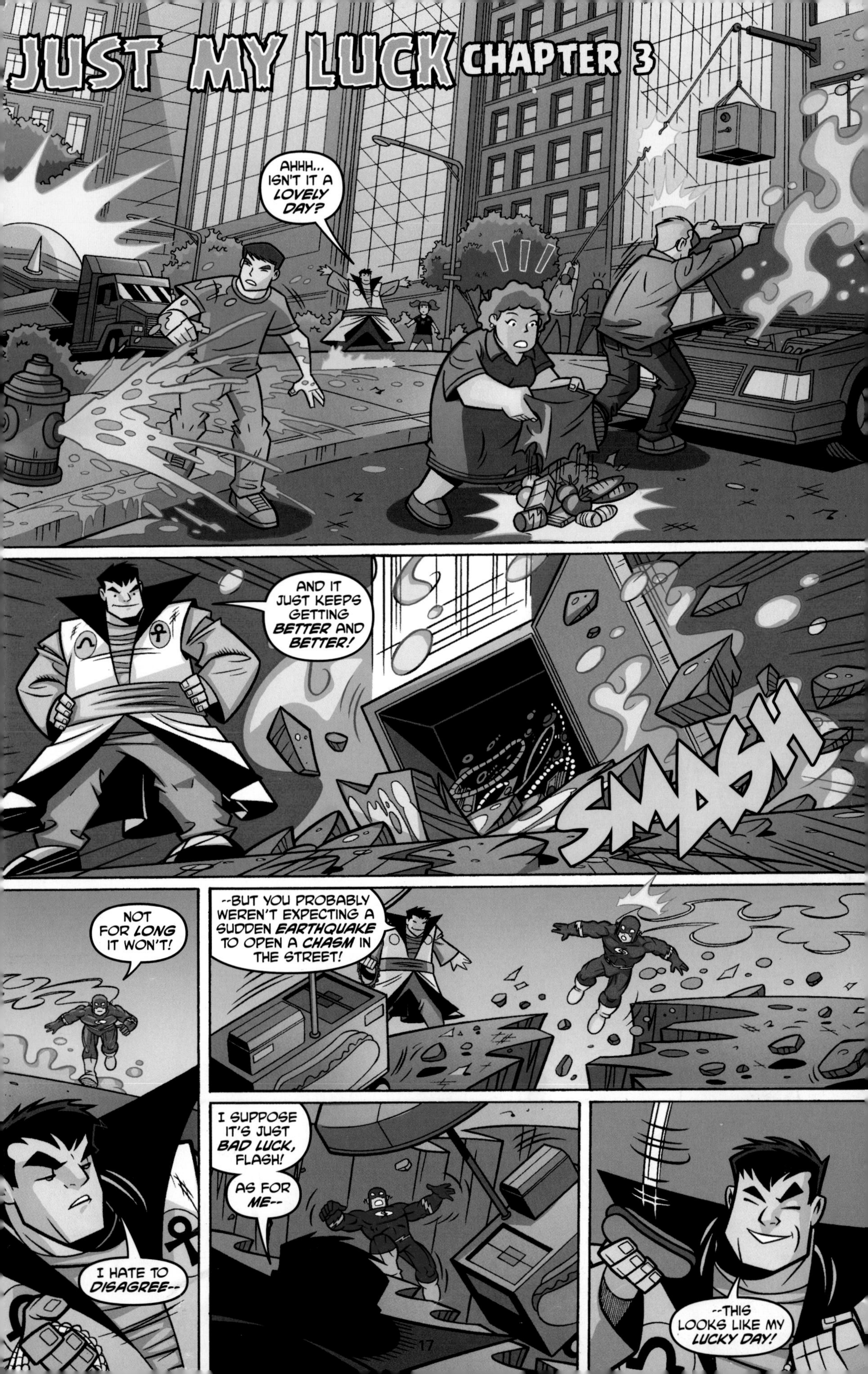
JUST MY LUCK CHAPTER 3
AHHH... ISN'T IT A LOVELY DAY?
AND IT JUST KEEPS GETTING BETTER AND BETTER!
SMASH
NOT FOR LONG IT WON'T!
--BUT YOU PROBABLY WEREN'T EXPECTING A SUDDEN EARTHQUAKE TO OPEN A CHASM IN THE STREET!
I HATE TO DISAGREE--
I SUPPOSE IT'S JUST BAD LUCK, FLASH!
AS FOR ME--
--THIS LOOKS LIKE MY LUCKY DAY!

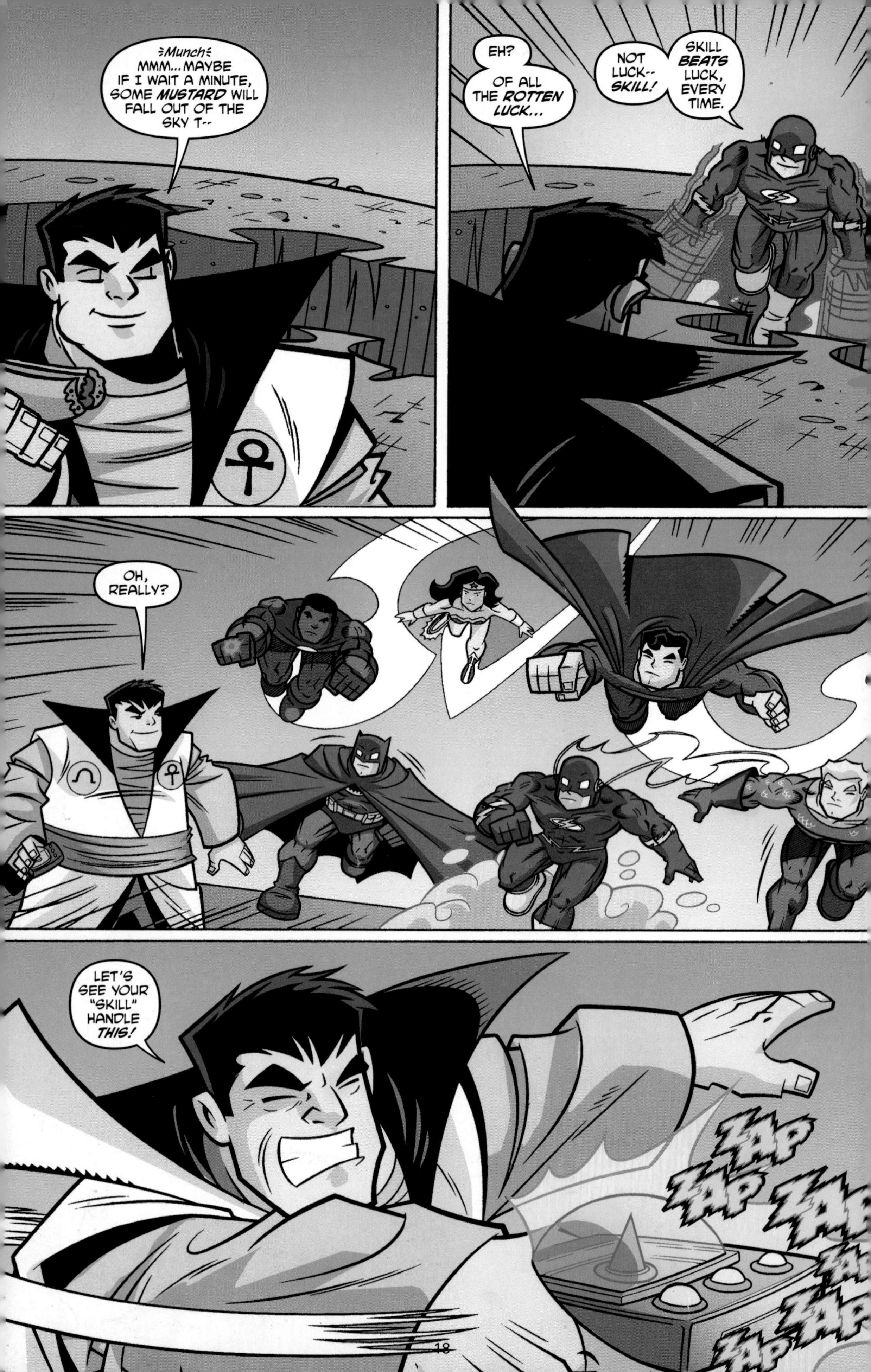

Munch
MMM... MAYBE IF I WAIT A MINUTE, SOME MUSTARD WILL FALL OUT OF THE SKY T--
EH?
OF ALL THE ROTTEN LUCK...
NOT LUCK-- SKILL!
SKILL BEATS LUCK, EVERY TIME.
OH, REALLY?
LET'S SEE YOUR "SKILL" HANDLE THIS!
ZAP ZAP ZAP ZAP ZAP ZAP

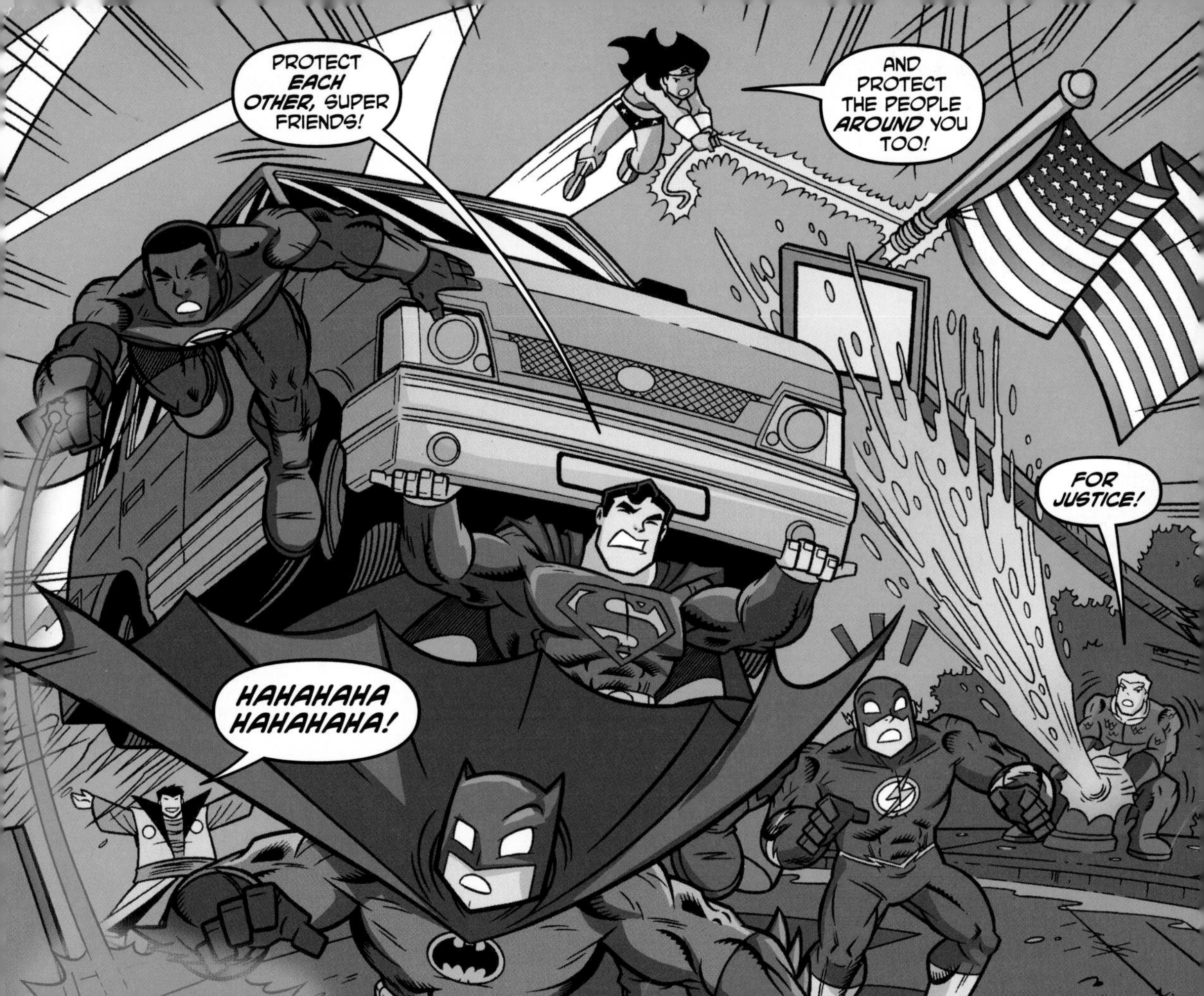
PROTECT EACH OTHER, SUPER FRIENDS!
AND PROTECT THE PEOPLE AROUND YOU TOO!
FOR JUSTICE!
HAHAHAHA HAHAHAHA!

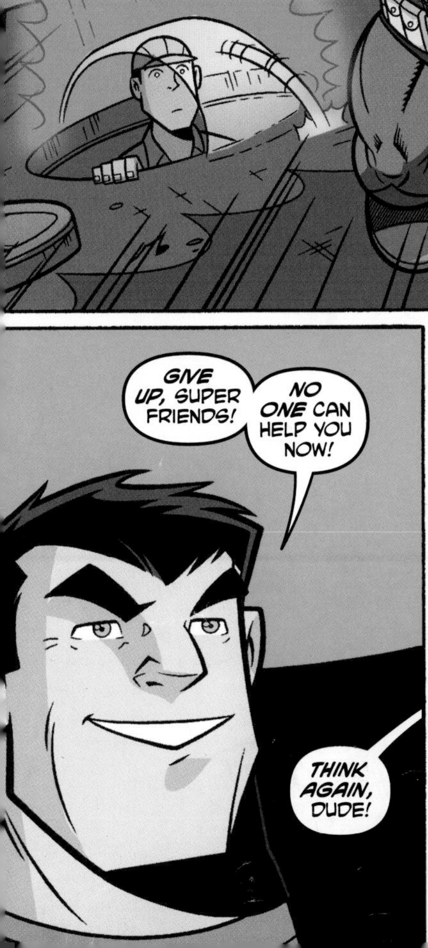
GIVE UP, SUPER FRIENDS!
NO ONE CAN HELP YOU NOW!
THINK AGAIN, DUDE!

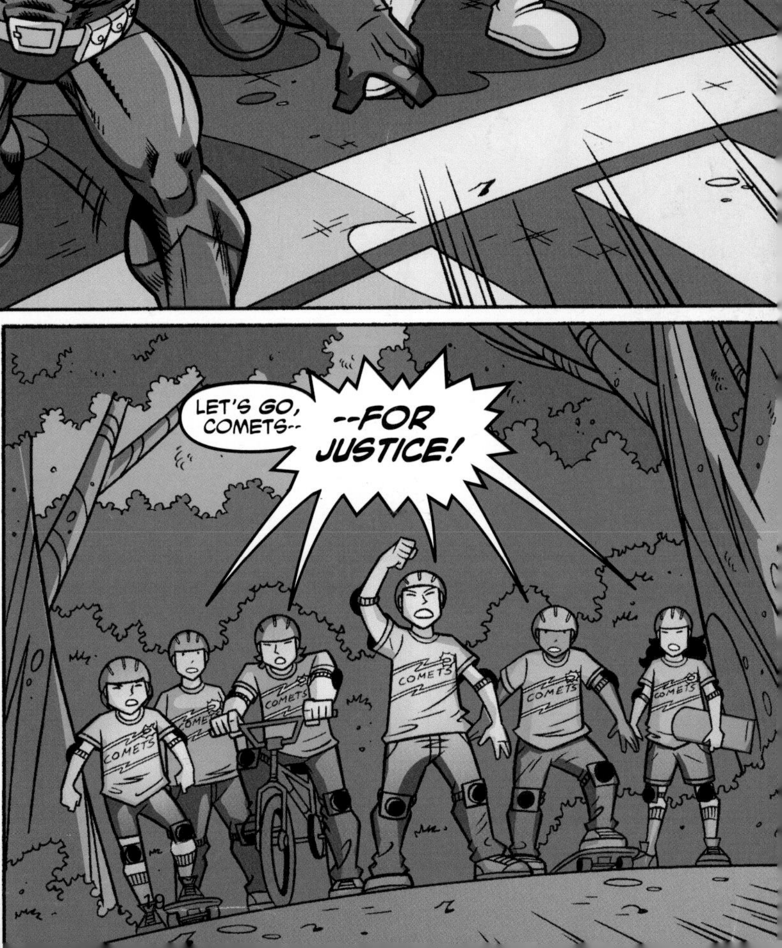
LET'S GO, COMETS--
--FOR JUSTICE!
COMETS

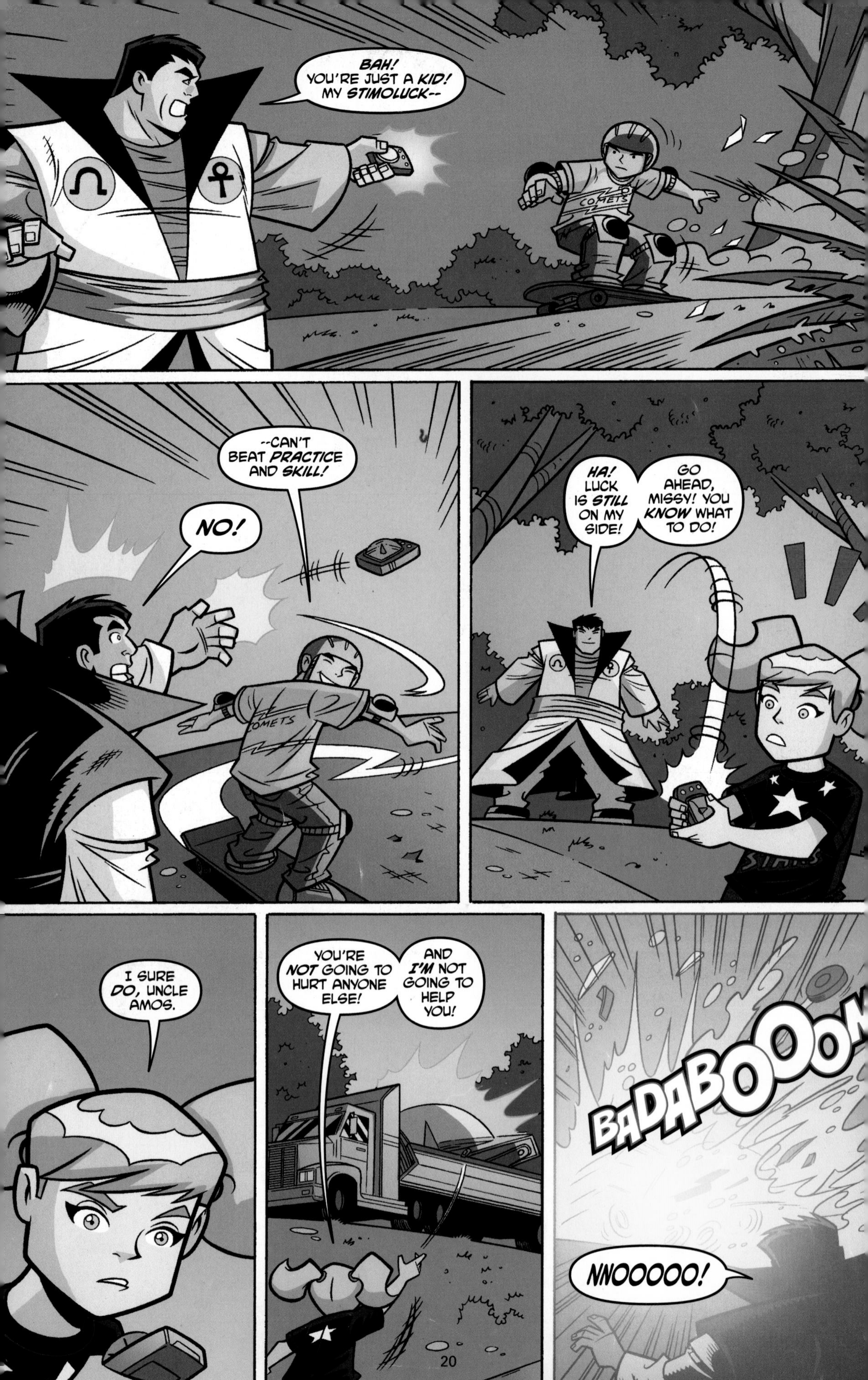
BAH! YOU'RE JUST A KID! MY STIMOLUCK--
--CAN'T BEAT PRACTICE AND SKILL!
NO!
HA! LUCK IS STILL ON MY SIDE!
GO AHEAD, MISSY! YOU KNOW WHAT TO DO!
I SURE DO, UNCLE AMOS.
YOU'RE NOT GOING TO HURT ANYONE ELSE!
AND I'M NOT GOING TO HELP YOU!
BADABOOOOM
NNOOOOO!

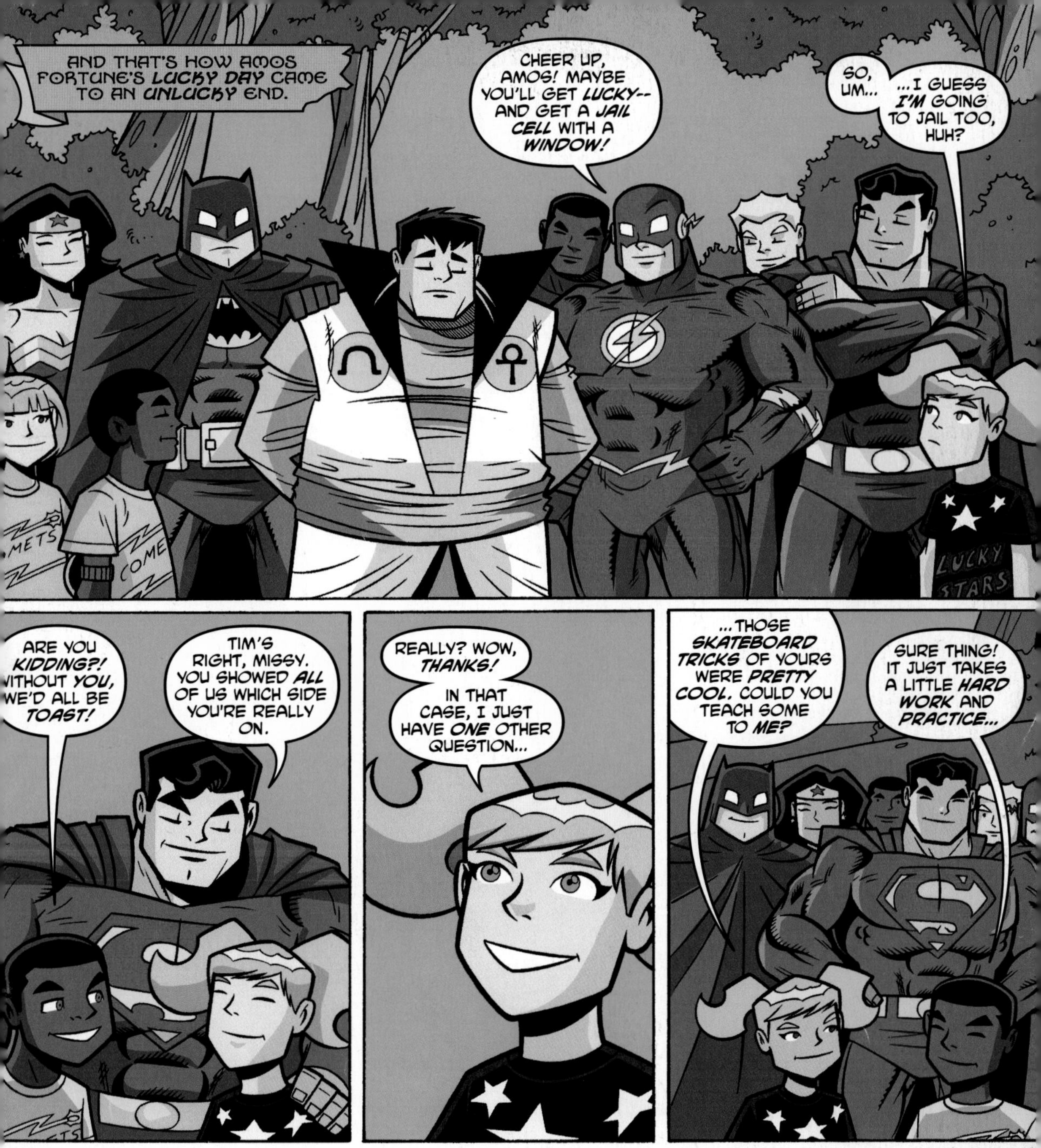
AND THAT'S HOW AMOS FORTUNE'S LUCKY DAY CAME TO AN UNLUCKY END.
CHEER UP, AMOS! MAYBE YOU'LL GET LUCKY-- AND GET A JAIL CELL WITH A WINDOW!
SO, UM...
...I GUESS I'M GOING TO JAIL TOO, HUH?
METS
COME
LUCKY STARS
ARE YOU KIDDING?! WITHOUT YOU, WE'D ALL BE TOAST!
TIM'S RIGHT, MISSY. YOU SHOWED ALL OF US WHICH SIDE YOU'RE REALLY ON.
REALLY? WOW, THANKS!
IN THAT CASE, I JUST HAVE ONE OTHER QUESTION...
...THOSE SKATEBOARD TRICKS OF YOURS WERE PRETTY COOL. COULD YOU TEACH SOME TO ME?
SURE THING! IT JUST TAKES A LITTLE HARD WORK AND PRACTICE...

ATTENTION, ALL SUPER FRIENDS!

HERE'S THIS BOOK'S SECRET MESSAGE:

PEVOY CYSOXRP ZBBU BEI CBY BINOYP

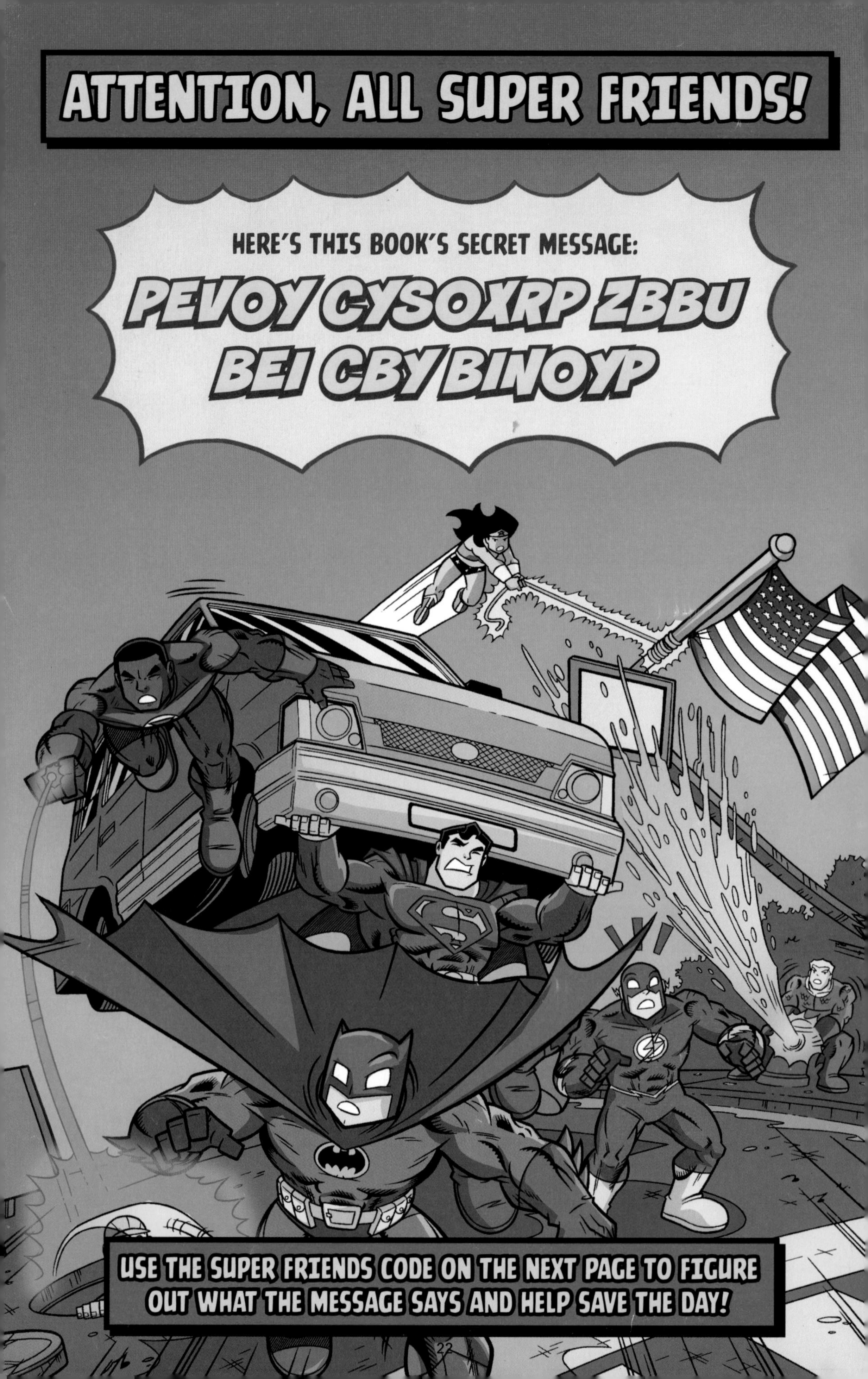

USE THE SUPER FRIENDS CODE ON THE NEXT PAGE TO FIGURE OUT WHAT THE MESSAGE SAYS AND HELP SAVE THE DAY!

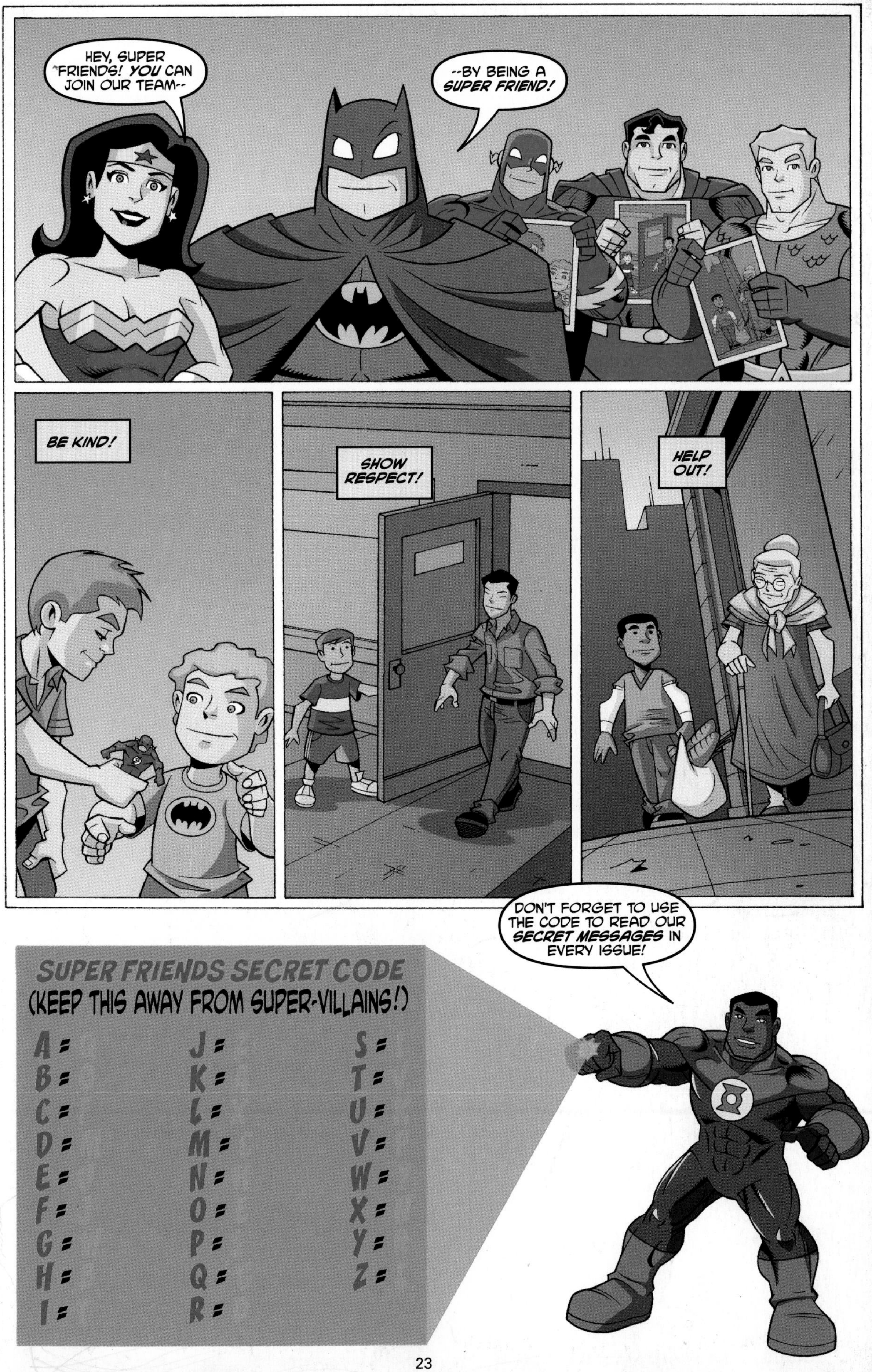
HEY, SUPER FRIENDS! YOU CAN JOIN OUR TEAM--
--BY BEING A SUPER FRIEND!
BE KIND!
SHOW RESPECT!
HELP OUT!
DON'T FORGET TO USE THE CODE TO READ OUR SECRET MESSAGES IN EVERY ISSUE!
SUPER FRIENDS SECRET CODE
(KEEP THIS AWAY FROM SUPER-VILLAINS!)
A =
B =
C =
D =
E =
F =
G =
H =
I =
J =
K =
L =
M =
N =
O =
P =
Q =
R =
S =
T =
U =
V =
W =
X =
Y =
Z =

KNOW YOUR SUPER FRIENDS!

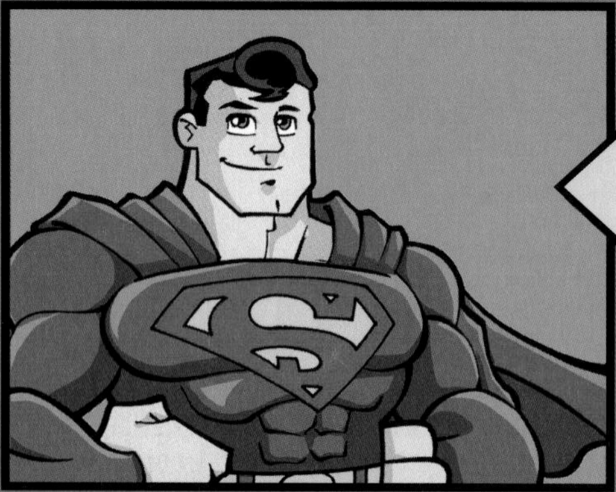

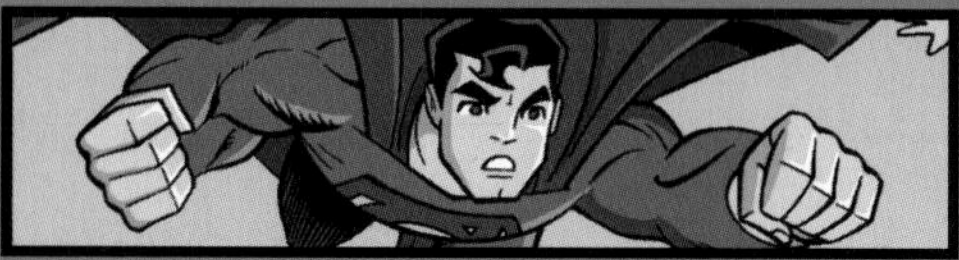

SUPERMAN

Real Name: Clark Kent

Powers: Super-strength, super-speed, flight, super-senses, heat vision, invulnerability, super-breath

Origin: Just before the planet Krypton exploded, baby Kal-EL escaped in a rocket to Earth. On Earth, he was adopted by a kind couple named Jonathan and Martha Kent.

BATMAN

Secret Identity: Bruce Wayne

Abilities: World's greatest detective, acrobat, escape artist

Origin: Orphaned at a young age, young millionaire Bruce Wayne promised to keep all people safe from crime. After training for many years, he put on costume that would scare criminals - the costume of Batman.

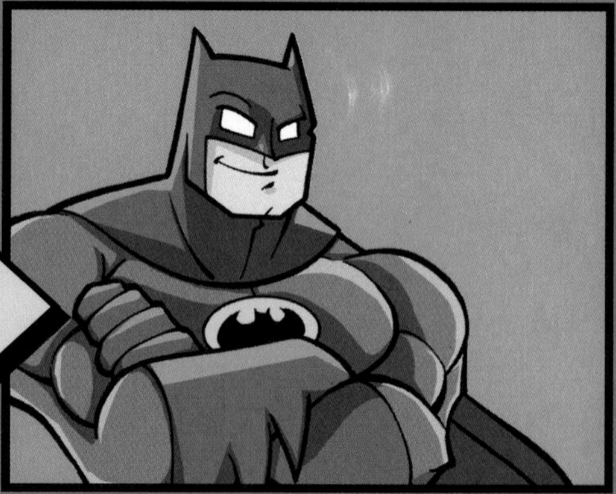

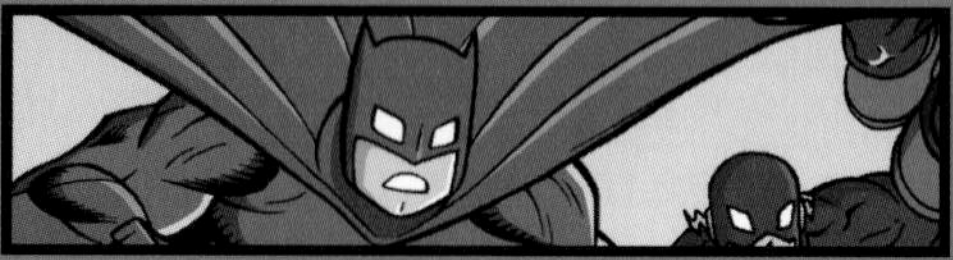

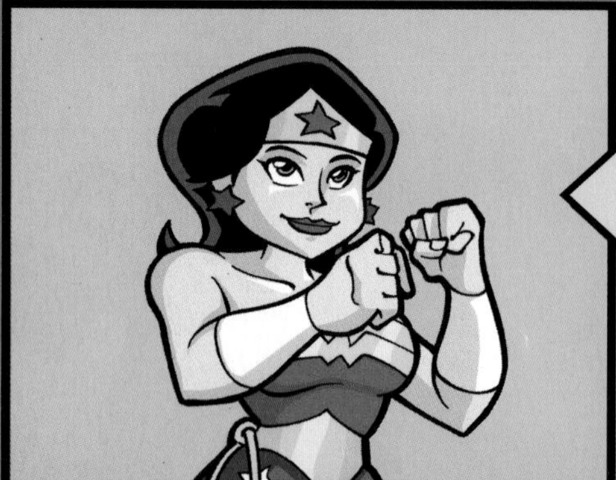

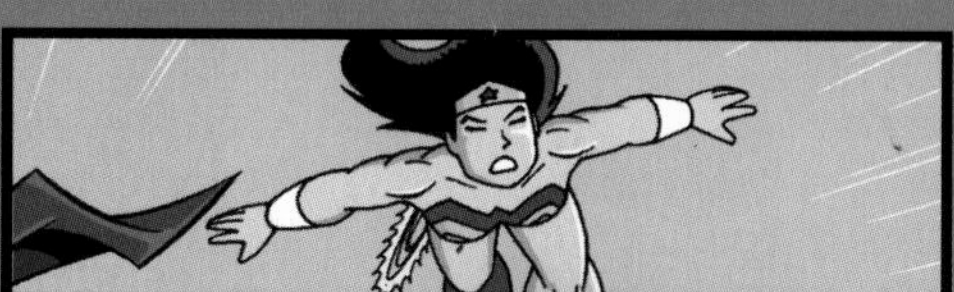

WONDER WOMAN

Secret Identity: Princess Diana

Powers: Super-strong, faster than normal humans, uses her bracelets as shields and magic lasso to make people tell the truth

Origin: Diana is the Princess of Paradise Island, the hidden home of the Amazons. When Diana was a baby, the Greek gods gave her special powers.

GREEN LANTERN

Secret Identity: John Stewart

Powers: Through the strength of willpower, Green Lantern's power ring can create anything he imagines

Origin: Led by the Guardians of the Universe, the Green Lantern Corps is an outer-space police force that keeps the whole universe safe. The Guardians chose John to protect Earth as our planet's Green Lantern.

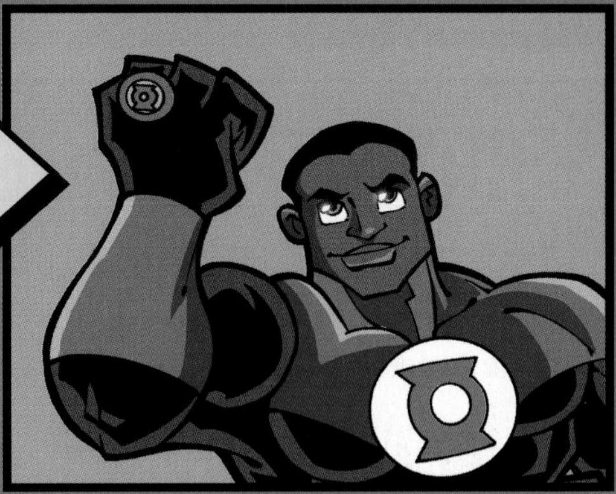

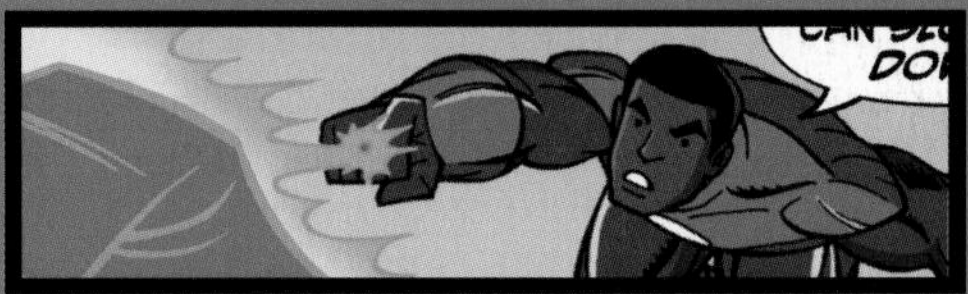

THE FLASH

Secret Identity: Wally West

Powers: Flash uses his super-speed in many ways: he can run across water or up the side of a building, spin around to make a tornado, or vibrate his body to walk right through a wall

Origin: As a boy, Wally West became the super-fast Kid Flash when lightning hit a rack of chemicals that spilled on him. Today, he helps others as the Flash.

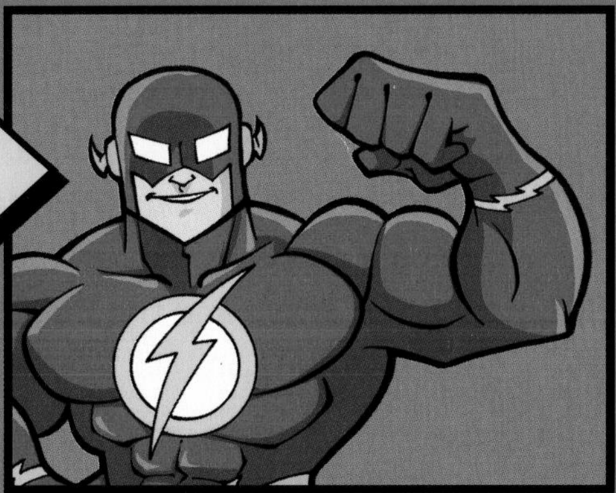

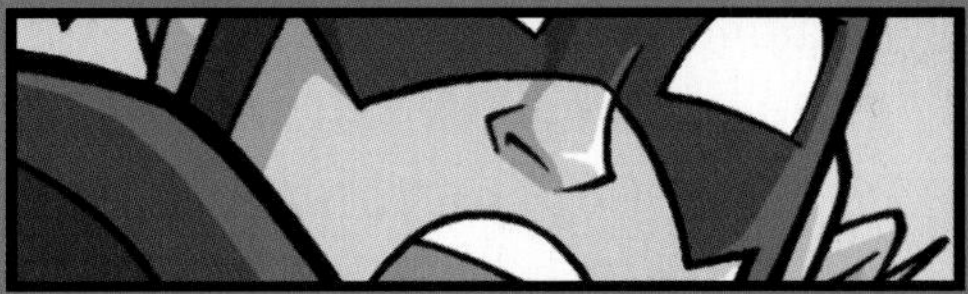

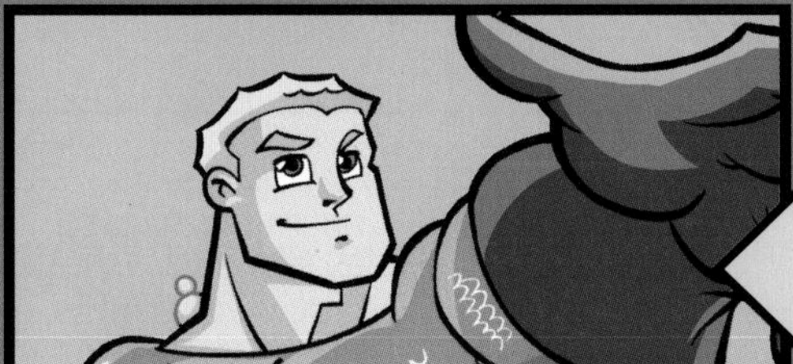

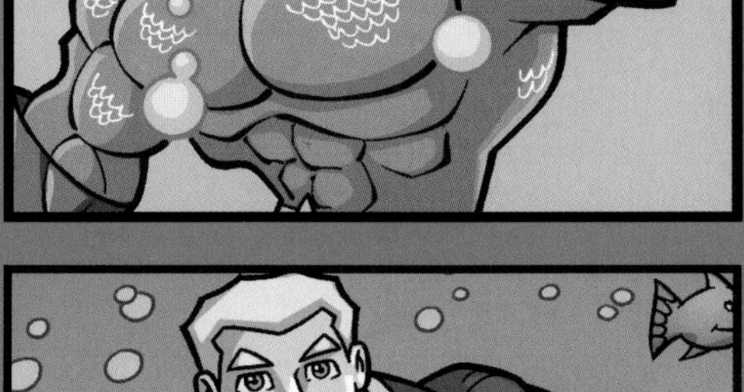

AQUAMAN

Real Name: King Orin or Arthur Curry

Powers: Breathes underwater, communicates with fish, swims at high speed, stronger than normal humans

Origin: Orin's father was a lighthouse keeper and his mother was a mermaid from the undersea land of Atlantis. As Orin grew up, he learned that he could live on land and underwater. He decided to use his powers to keep the seven seas safe as Aquaman.

CREATORS

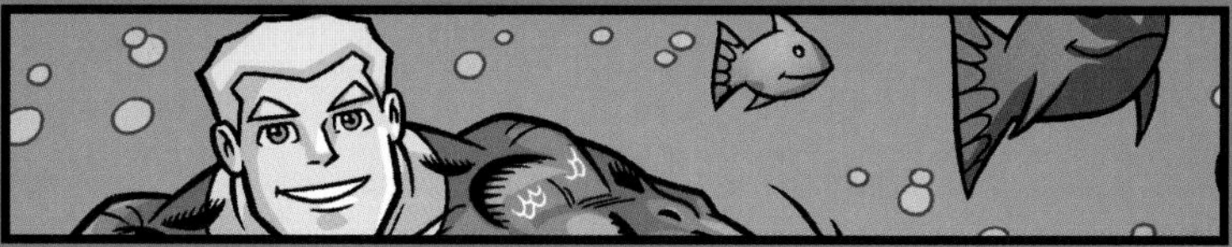

SHOLLY FISCH WRITER

Bitten by a radioactive typewriter, Sholly Fisch has spent the wee hours writing books, comics, TV scripts, and online material for more than 25 years. His comic book credits include more than 200 stories and features about characters such as Batman, Superman, Bugs Bunny, Daffy Duck, Spider-Man, and Ben 10. Currently, he writes stories for Action Comics every month, plus stories for Looney Tunes and Scooby-Doo. By day, Sholly is a mild-mannered developmental psychologist who helps to create educational TV shows, web sites, and other media for kids.

DARIO BRIZUELA ARTIST

Dario Brizuela is a professional comic book artist. He's illustrated some of today's most popular characters, including Batman, Green Lantern, Teenage Mutant Ninja Turtles, Thor, Iron Man, and Transformers. His best-known works for DC Comics include the series DC Super Friends, Justice League Unlimited, and Batman: The Brave and the Bold.

J. BONE COVER ARTIST

J.Bone is a Toronto based illustrator and comic book artist. Besides DC Super Friends, he has worked on comic books such as Spiderman: Tangled Web, Mr. Gum, Gotham Girls, and Madman Adventures. He is also the co-creator of the Alison Dare comic book series.

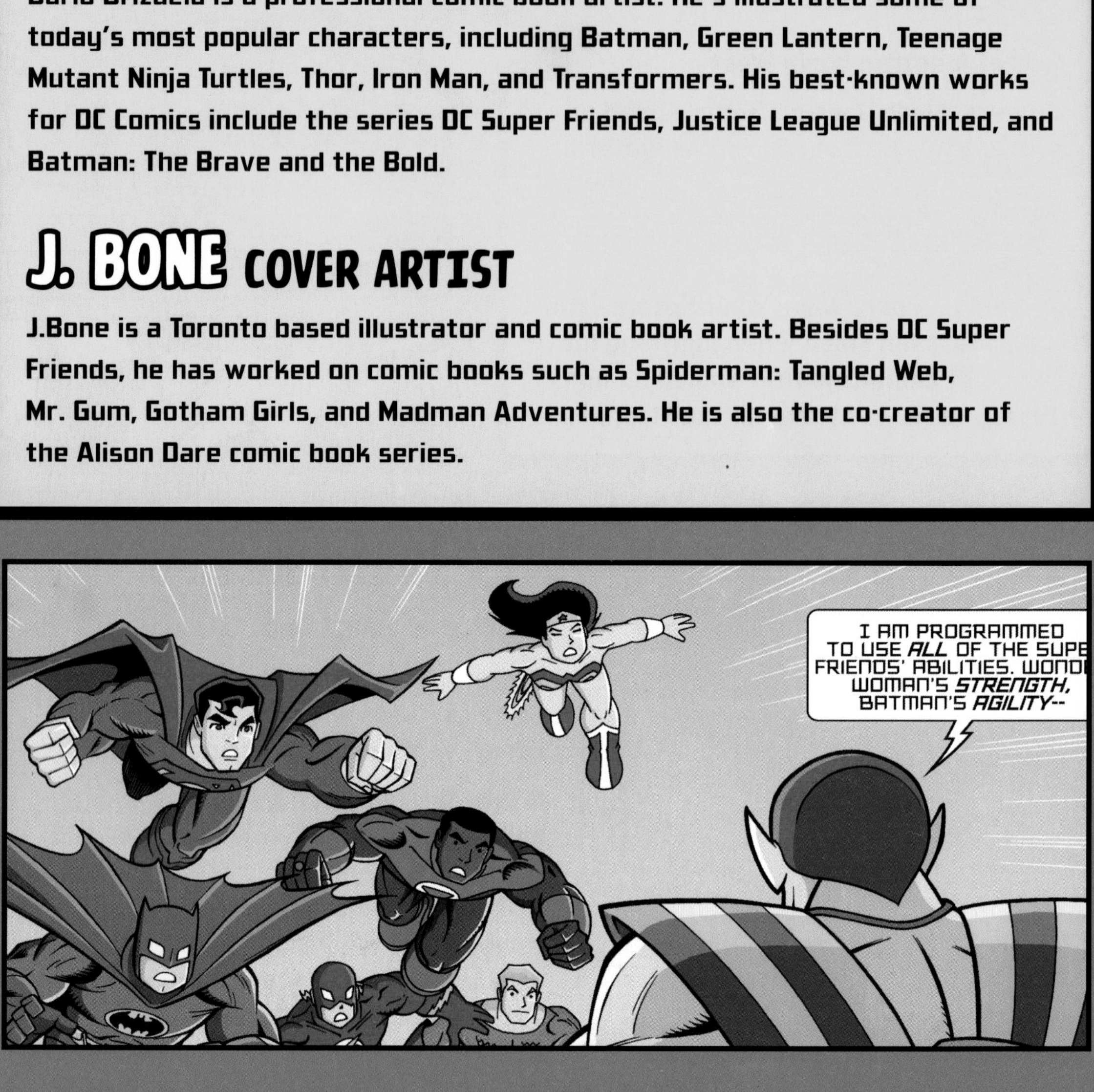
I AM PROGRAMMED TO USE ALL OF THE SUPE FRIENDS' ABILITIES. WOND WOMAN'S STRENGTH, BATMAN'S AGILITY--

GLOSSARY

accidents [AK-si-duhnts]-unfortunate and unplanned events

championship [CHAM-pee-uhn-ship]-a contest or final game of a series that determines which team or player will be the overall winner

chasm [KAZ-uhm]-a deep crack in the surface of the earth

citywide [SIT-ee-WIDE]-including or throughout an entire city

competition [kom-puh-TISH-uhn]-a contest of some kind

dangerous [DAYN-jur-uhss]-not safe, or likely to cause harm or injury

develop [di-VEL-uhp]-to build on something, or to make something grow

earthquake [URTH-kwayk]-a sudden, violent shaking of the earth caused by a shifting of the earth's crust

half pipe [HAF PIPE]-a U-shaped ramp, usually with a flat section in the middle

nonsense [NON-senss]-silly or without meaning

rigging [RIG-ing]-controlling something dishonestly

vision [VIZH-uhn]-the sense of sight

MY POWER RI
CAN SLOW HI
DOWN!

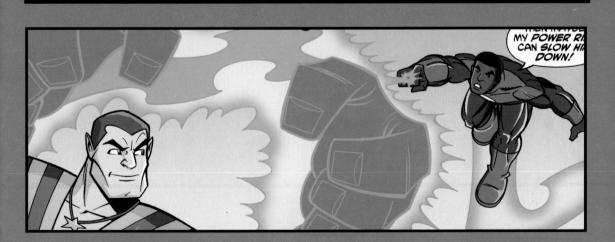

VISUAL QUESTIONS & PROMPTS

1. Explain how Amos, the character on the right, is feeling. What are some visual clues that support your answer?

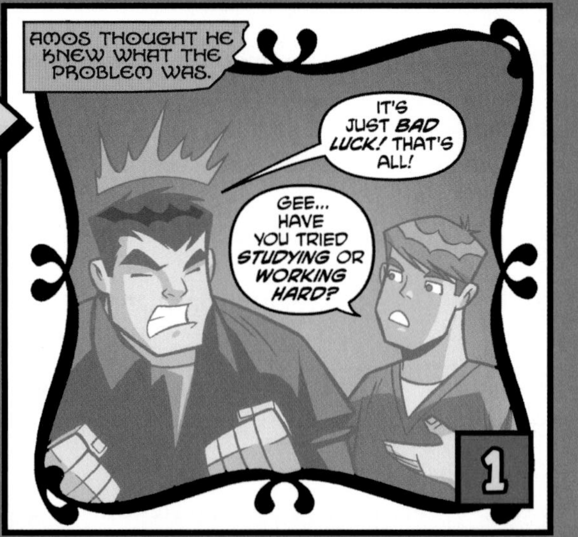

AMOS THOUGHT HE KNEW WHAT THE PROBLEM WAS.
IT'S JUST *BAD LUCK!* THAT'S ALL!
GEE... HAVE YOU TRIED *STUDYING* OR *WORKING HARD?*
1

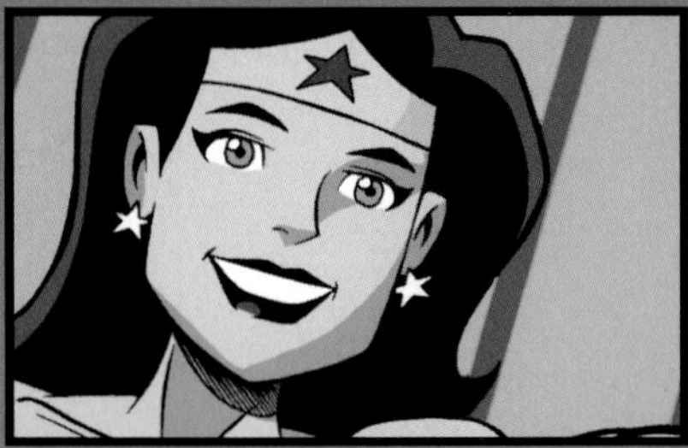

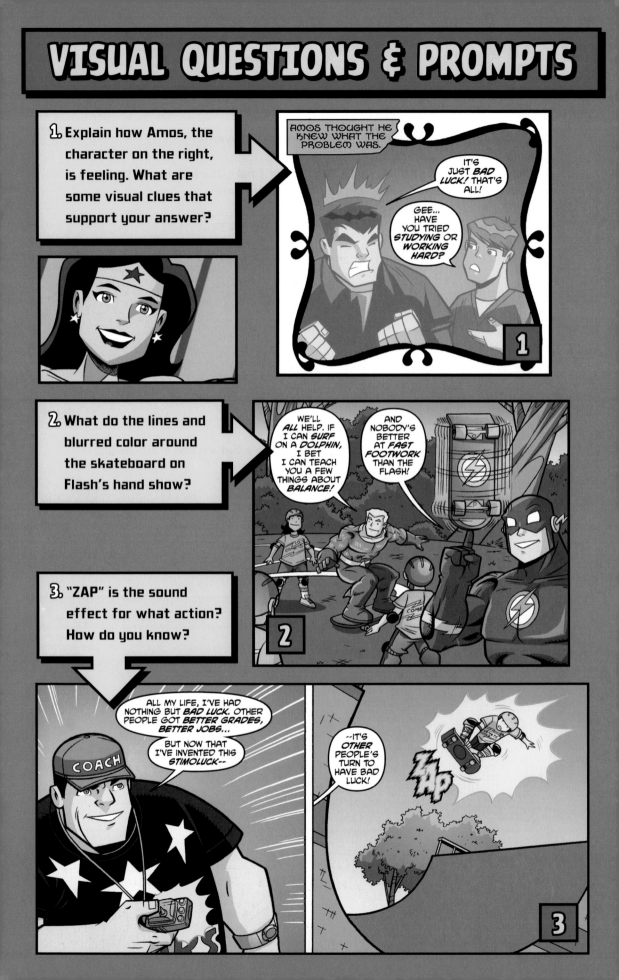

2. What do the lines and blurred color around the skateboard on Flash's hand show?

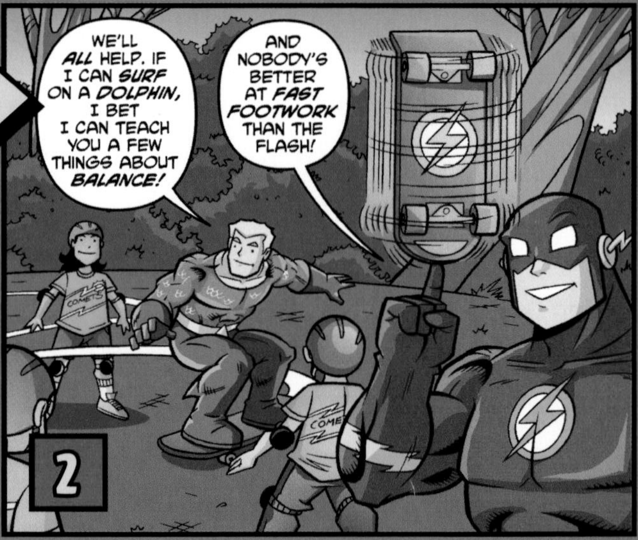

WE'LL *ALL* HELP. IF I CAN *SURF* ON A *DOLPHIN,* I BET I CAN TEACH YOU A FEW THINGS ABOUT *BALANCE!*
AND NOBODY'S BETTER AT *FAST FOOTWORK* THAN THE FLASH!
2

3. "ZAP" is the sound effect for what action? How do you know?

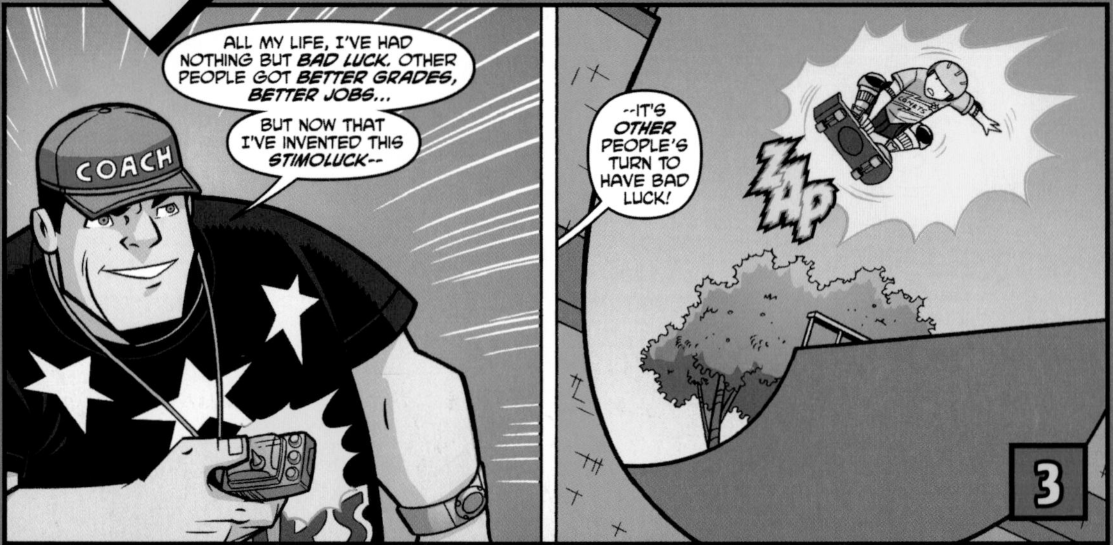

ALL MY LIFE, I'VE HAD NOTHING BUT *BAD LUCK.* OTHER PEOPLE GOT *BETTER GRADES, BETTER JOBS...*
BUT NOW THAT I'VE INVENTED THIS *STIMOLUCK--*
COACH
--IT'S *OTHER* PEOPLE'S TURN TO HAVE BAD LUCK!
ZAP
3

4. What examples of bad luck do you see in this panel?

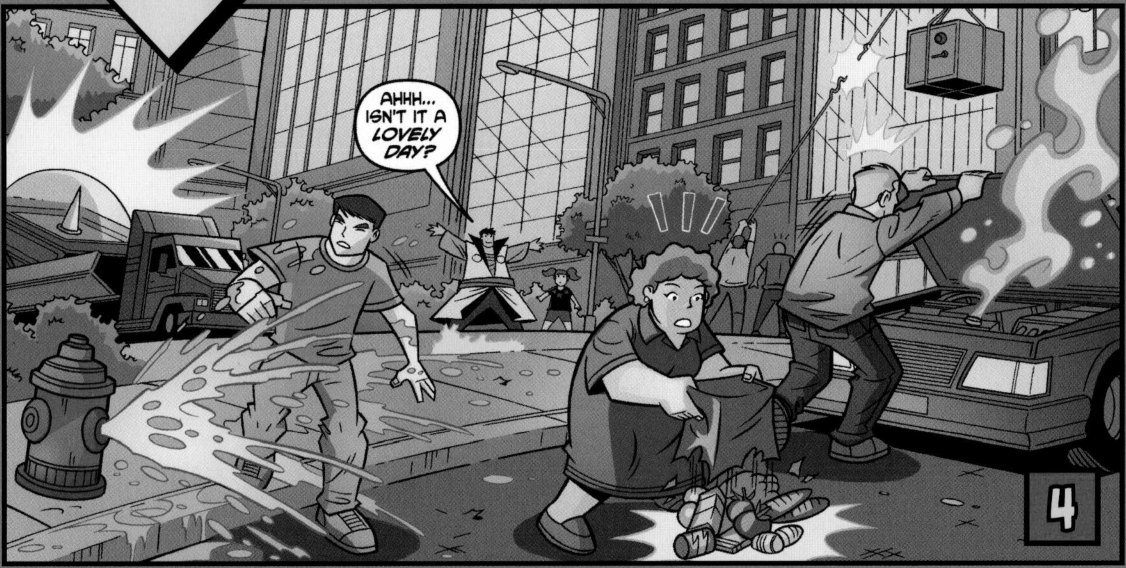
AHHH... ISN'T IT A *LOVELY DAY?*
4

5. This single panel shows a series of actions. Can you explain them in order?

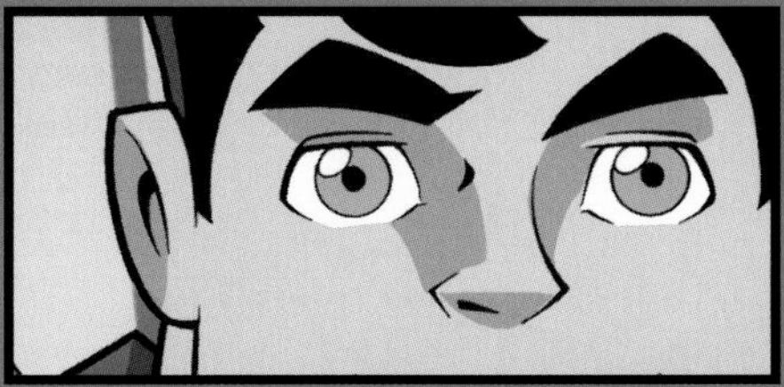

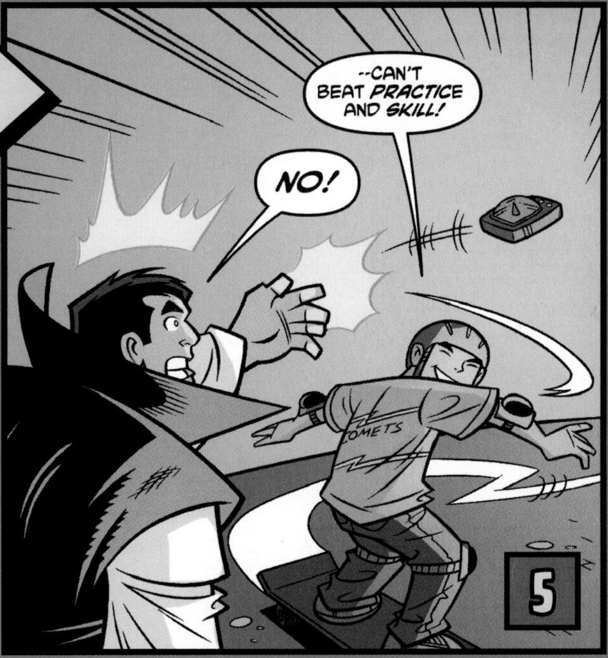
--CAN'T BEAT *PRACTICE* AND *SKILL!*
NO!
COMETS
5

6. This panel shows the stimoluck cannon exploding, emphasized by a large sound effect word. What other sound effect words could the artist have used here?

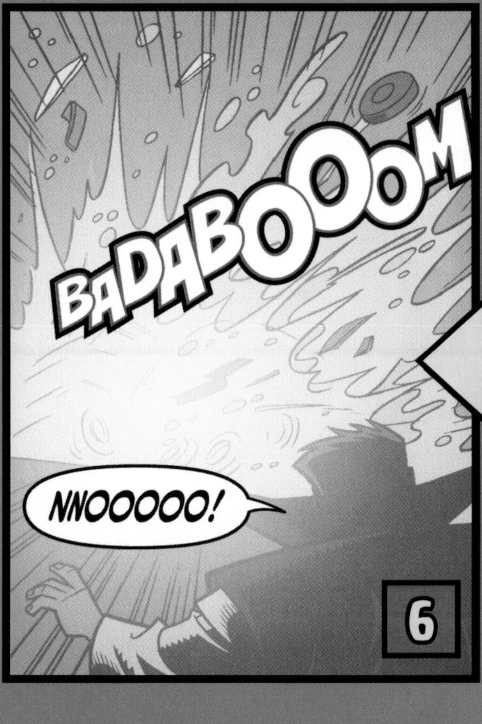
BADABOOOOM
NNOOOOO!
6

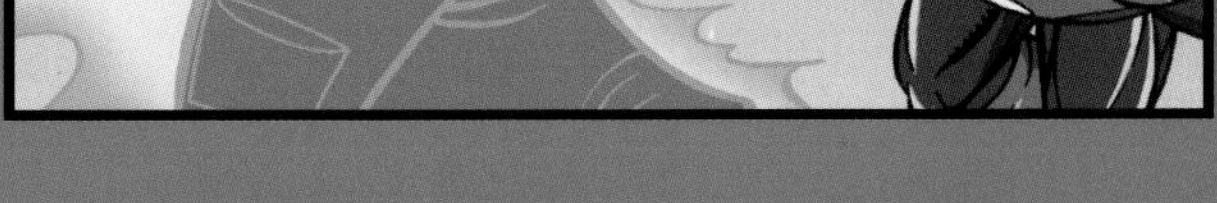

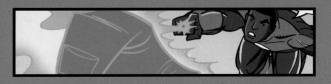

READ THEM ALL!

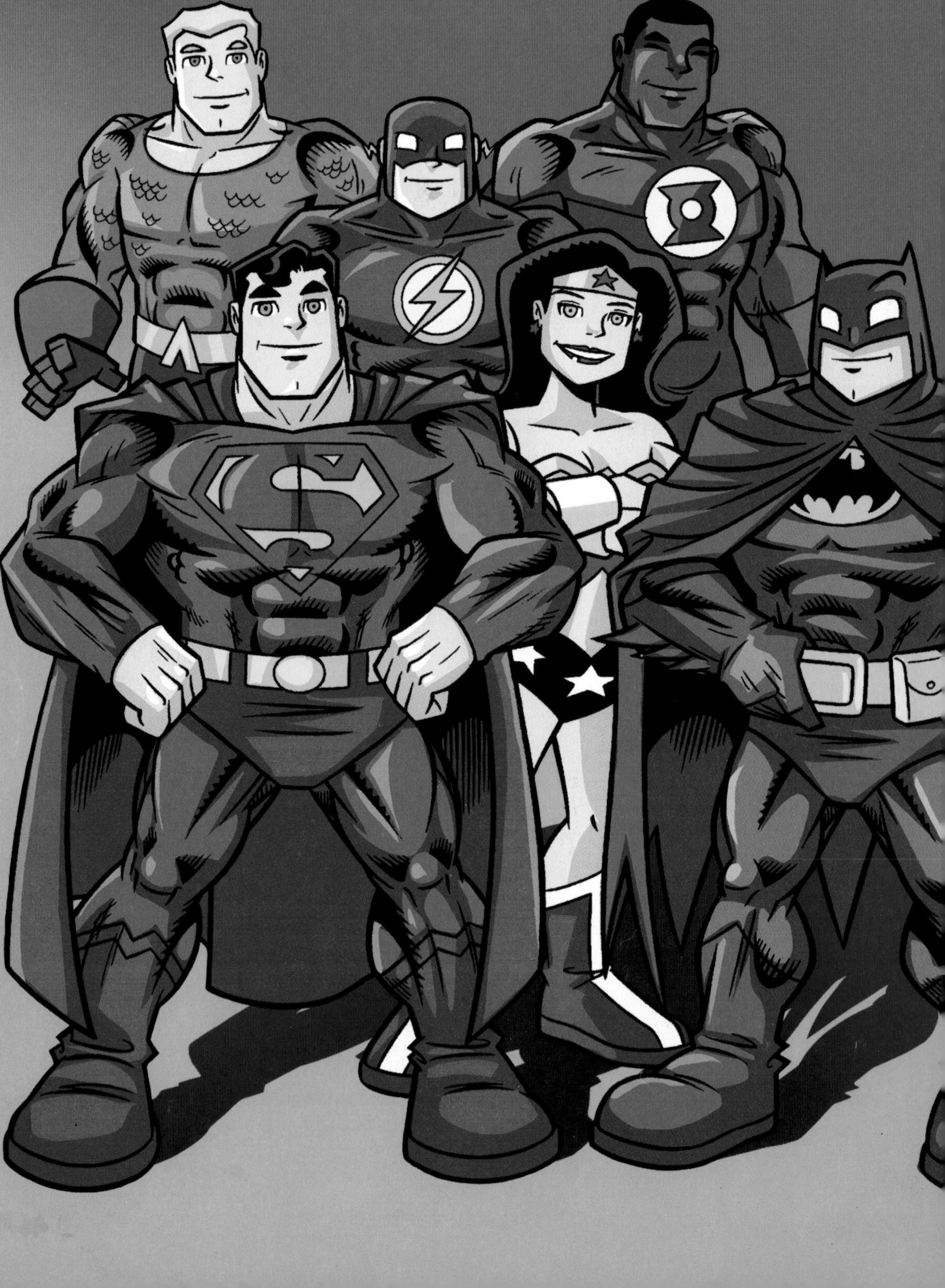

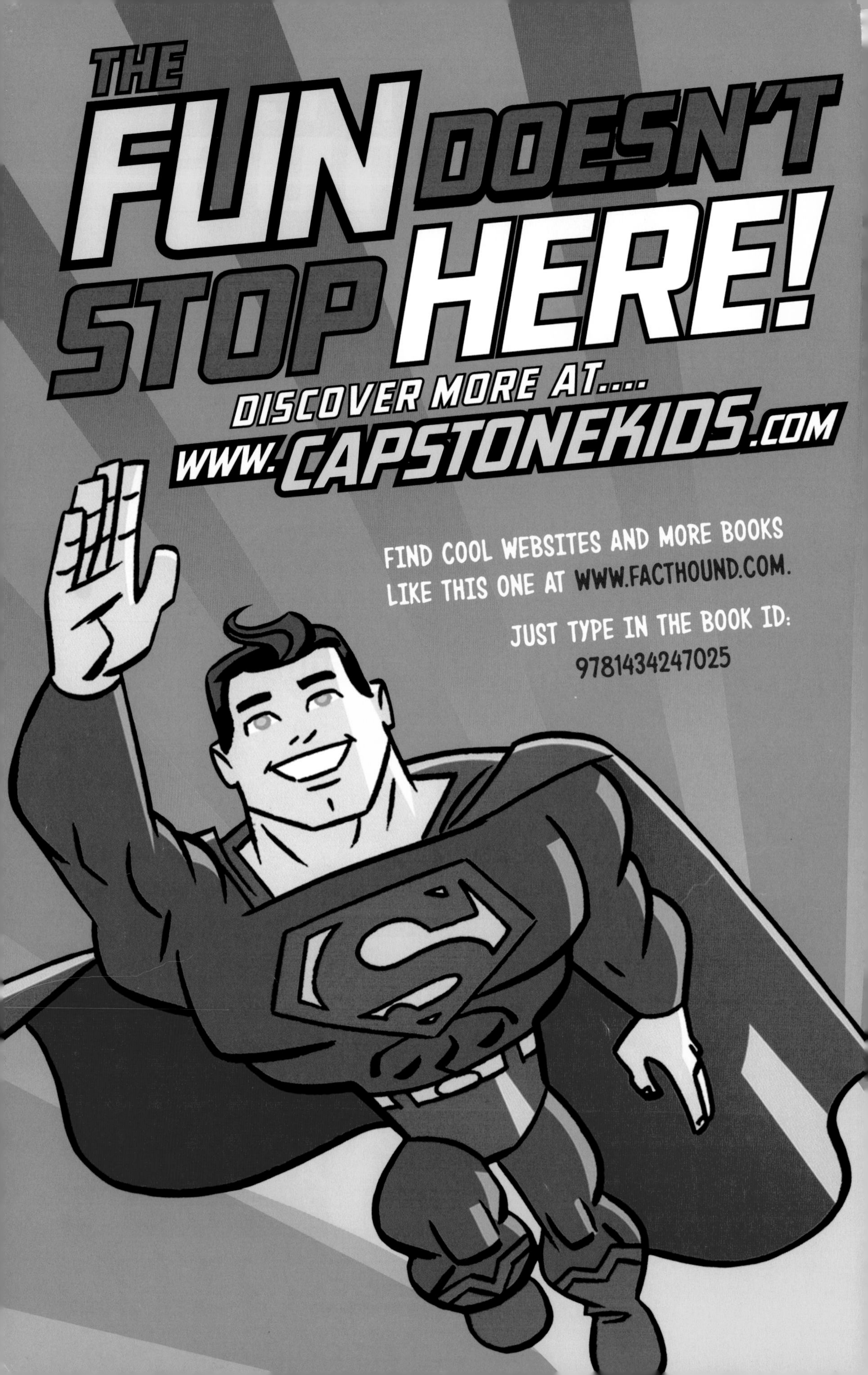
THE FUN DOESN'T STOP HERE!
DISCOVER MORE AT....
WWW.CAPSTONEKIDS.COM
FIND COOL WEBSITES AND MORE BOOKS LIKE THIS ONE AT WWW.FACTHOUND.COM.
JUST TYPE IN THE BOOK ID:
9781434247025